Best wishes
Enjoy!
John Platt

GW00391133

JAN PENDRAY

(BOOK ONE)

by John Platts

CHAPTER 1

The hurt Jan felt as he mounted his horse was too much to bear. Blindly he guided his charge out of the courtyard, down the tree-lined drive and onto the deserted road, leaving behind the towering gates and a host of painful memories.

The turmoil in the rider was immediately transferred to the horse which set out across the barren hillside with reckless abandon. A full hour later, Jan Pendray allowed the animal to slow, aware of the foaming sweat that poured down its hind quarters and the hot steam that snorted forth from its flared nostrils. Still the feeling of hurt tore into him. He dismounted and sat on one of the granite outcrops that littered the area in grand profusion. Lowering his head into his hands he began to cry. The long drawn out sobs echoing from his aching heart were in sharp contrast to the eerie silence that surrounded this remote part of Cornwall. His sobbing continued until all his emotional strength had gone.

"If only I had money and station," he thought wildly. "I know she loves me."

But the grounds for a suitable match were lost to a mixture of prestige, wealth and parental disapproval. Love could provide little comfort against such overwhelming odds.

The sun was setting over the distant hills when he remounted and trotted slowly towards Falmouth. His spirit had been broken and his heart torn apart, it would take a long time for the wounds to heal. As he approached the outskirts of Penryn, the road dropped steeply into a dark, tree-lined alley. He dismounted and led the ailing horse carefully through the avenue of trees, anxious not to cause injury in the deep ruts that had been fashioned by the wheels of the carriages that passed that way on the journey to town. Just as he was approaching the end of the avenue he became aware of a commotion taking place further down the road. At first the dimness obscured any hope of observing what was amiss but, as he drew closer, he was able to pick out the cause of the disturbance.

Three vagabonds dressed in rags were setting about a man. Two had clubs and Jan noted the ominous glint of cold steel in the hand of the third. There was little doubt that the three assailants were inflicting heavy punishment on the poor unfortunate soul who was lying on the ground with blood pouring from a nasty cut on his forehead. Jan needed only a second to assess the situation, with the yell of a man possessed, he jumped into the fray both fists flailing showing a complete disregard for the superior numbers of the attackers. His clenched fist sunk into the nearest man's stomach with such a fury that it knocked him off balance leaving him on the ground gasping for breath. The other two quickly turned to face their new foe, confident that the odds were still in their favour. However, they were not aware of the frenzy that burned in Jan. He hurled himself at the two men with such vigour that he caught them off guard, knocking one of the clubs to the ground. His advantage was only temporary, with a volume of curses they sprang back and pinned him to the floor. He felt a sickening pain as a well- aimed boot caught him full on the side, quickly followed by a shower of punches to the head. He began to feel the strength drain from him as he wilted under the barrage of heavy blows. He sensed his body drifting away as he slipped into a state of semi-consciousness. He was only dimly aware of what happened next.

The man who had been beaten into submission had managed to struggle to his feet and grab the club that Jan had knocked from the hand of one of the attackers. Choosing his moment well, he brought it crashing down on to the skull of the man who was pinning Jan to the floor. The unfortunate wretch crumpled in a heap without uttering a sound. The last man, realising that the odds were now reversed, took flight and ran off into the gathering darkness.

Jan struggled to his feet and the two men looked at one another for the first time.

"I think I owe you a good deal of thanks," said the stranger as he gulped in welcome air.

"It is I who should thank you," Jan replied with a smile. "It may seem strange but I feel much better than I did an hour ago."

The stranger eyed Jan's battered appearance with a wry grin but he made no comment aware that some inner force had been working inside the young man which had been much to his advantage.

After inspecting each other for a few moments both were able to report that the damage to their persons was only of a superficial nature although the stranger did have a nasty gash on his forehead.

"Where are you bound?" He asked Jan as he brushed the dust from his breeches.

"I rent a room in Falmouth but I have no cause or even inclination to return to it at present."

"In that case, how would you like to accompany me to my home? It is 7 miles as the crow flies, I would be glad of your company."

Jan stared at the stranger with interest. He was older than him with an air of breeding, but his clothes and general demeanour were plain. Falmouth provided little by way of comfort, just an empty room and a host of memories that had gone sour. He did not take long to make up his mind.

"Aye, I'll come with you, I have nothing else left in the world, so the direction I take matters little."

The two men shook hands and a silent bond was established that was to last for a very long time.

CHAPTER 2

The hill out of Penryn towards Helston was tortuous. The poor nag which Jan had managed to recover after the struggle, heaved and coughed as it bore the two men slowly away from civilisation and on to the open road. For a while both men were silent, each lost in their own thoughts.

Jan thought back to his childhood. He was now twenty-one but already his life had been one of insecurity and near starvation. His mother had died in childbirth, a shock from which his father never recovered- they had been married barely a year. Jan was forced to face the harsh realities of life from an early age. Although his father tried hard to compensate for the loss of his mother, it was impossible for him to find time to bring up a child. Sheer necessity forced him to continue fishing. The alternative was starvation for him and his child. The enforced solitude bred into Jan's character a keen sense of independence and from a young age his father was hard-pressed to control his wilful streak. Despite the hardships they endured together there was a firm bond of love and affection and so it was a further crippling blow to the young boy when his father died when he was only sixteen.

Jan was heartbroken but he was now capable of standing on his own two feet. His father had left him virtually nothing in terms of material wealth but, instead, something far more valuable, a knowledge and understanding of the sea .He was always on the dockside waiting for his father to return from Carrick Roads, excitement would fill his shining eyes as he saw the shimmering fish crowd the deck of his father's tiny boat. Soon he was allowed to accompany his father, learning how to bait lines, pull pots and manoeuvre the boat between the hulking galleons and Packet ships that furnished the trade of the busy port.

His lessons at the village school he endured. His mind was often way out to sea but surprisingly enough, when he left at fourteen, he had mastered the rudiments of Arithmetic and a better than average, command of the English language. Blessed with a sturdy body he was able to face most of the problems that life threw at him.

After an hour the horse was showing visible signs of exhaustion. A sharp tap on the shoulder interrupted his thoughts.

"The horse needs a rest."

Both men dismounted and started to walk. It was dark now, with big black clouds scudding across the sky obscuring most of the light from the moon and stars. The stranger seemed undeterred, picking his route with an air of confidence that filled Jan with admiration.

At length they were able to pick out the lights of the Half-way House Inn, its welcoming lantern shining warmly against the blackness of the sky.

"We can stop here for a while," the stranger said confidently. They tethered the horse on the rail outside and went through the narrow door.

Jan had heard of the Half-way House before and had often ridden past it but he had never dared to venture inside. Tales of highwaymen, smugglers and all manner of unseemly characters had been more than enough to dissipate his curiosity. On this occasion however, the stranger was so confident that Jan meekly followed him inside.

The room was dark apart from a candle placed on a table beside a large log fire. It offered welcome warmth to the travellers. Jan looked around with interest. By the glow of the fire and the small candle he was able to see that the room was empty apart from a large hairy dog that sprawled in front of the hearth. It ignored them both and showed no inclination to move. The walls were painted yellow and the low ceiling a light brown both were showing the effects of many years of tobacco smoke and stale beer. Despite its unkempt appearance, the room offered a degree of cosiness for which they were grateful. They pulled up a couple of high backed, leather chairs and made themselves comfortable by the fire. The dog managed to open one eye but did not stir.

A door in the far corner opened and a huge, gluttonous man waddled in.

"Thought I heard 'e Captain," he boomed, cleaning his hands on the apron that hung precariously around his waist.

The stranger acknowledged the greeting and ordered a jug of ale and a loaf of bread with cheese. The Innkeeper took the order with good grace and shuffled out. They sat in silence watching the flickering flames shoot out of the logs and disappear up the chimney. Jan's companion was the first to break the silence.

"My name is John Carter, what's yours?"

"Jan Pendray."

"Well Jan Pendray, 'tis woman trouble that's been worrying you, I'll be bound."

It was a statement, not a question so Jan remained silent. He was not yet ready to discuss his personal problems with a man he had known for little more than an hour. Instead he responded in a different vein.

"You know this place well, then?"

"Aye, I've had cause to stop here on a few occasions- the ale is good and the food is plain and wholesome. That's all I ask."

Jan was curious about his new friend. There was a certain bearing about John Carter that fascinated him. He was not particularly striking in stature, nor was his manner that of a gentleman but he possessed an aura that led one to believe he was quite capable of mixing in any class of society. Jan tried to guess his age but he could not, his weather beaten face may have been the result of a sea-going childhood which prematurely ages many a man. His hands were rough and scaly in contrast to the tight, delicate gestures of his fingers. But the most striking feature were his eyes, they changed with every movement of his face. One minute they would twinkle with amusement the next they would become cold and grey, they never stayed the same for long. Despite his rough exterior, Jan liked him although he was not sure he entirely trusted him.

His deliberations were cut short by the arrival of a serving maid carrying a large jug of ale and two pewter mugs.

"Hello, Kate," said John Carter and stood up to let the girl reach the table.

"Hello Cap'n, nice to see you again- it's been a long time." A knowing look passed between them that was not lost on Jan.

"How's your father these days?"

"He's right fine thankee Cap'n, he is always asking after you."

"I shall make a point of calling on him soon and bring him some of his favourite, if he's a mind to drink it."

The girl laughed. "He'll do that alright."

They watched her go. Even in the gloom of the lounge they could see the ample curves of her body.

"A great lass is Kate," John murmured with affection before turning his attention to the jug of frothy beer that stood waiting on the table.

Both men gulped down the dark brown liquid enjoying the warm glow as it settled in the pit of their stomachs. As the beer flowed so the conversation increased, without realising it, Jan launched himself into an account of the chain of events that had occurred prior to his meeting John Carter.

John listened intently, nodding occasionally but saying nothing. When he had finished, Jan sat back in the leather chair rather surprised that he had told the whole story to a complete stranger.

"And what are you going to do now?" It was the first words he had spoken and it took Jan off guard.

"I don't know," he stammered. "I suppose I shall go in search of money and status and hope that she will wait for me."

"Money and status are no substitute for love, you already possess the richest commodity a man can have."

"But how am I going to persuade her father to give her hand in marriage to a penniless layabout?" Jan's voice cracked as he once again, realised the hopelessness of his quest.

"There, I agree with you. Are you certain she will continue to love you even when you are not around? Women are fickle creatures."

"I've never been so certain about anything in my life. If only circumstances were different."

"Circumstances can be changed, Jan, destiny cannot. If you are absolutely convinced this woman will wait for you, I may be able to help. I owe you a favour and 'The King of Prussia' never forgets."

Jan started. "Did you say 'The King of Prussia?'"

John Carter nodded. "Yes, that is who I am."

Jan's mouth fell open. 'The King of Prussia' was a legend along the South coast of Cornwall. His exploits of courage and daring were already a part of Cornish folklore. For years he had been bringing in illicit cargoes right under the noses of the Excise men. He had never been caught.

He was regarded as invincible. Often Jan's father had told him stories of an outlaw who had roamed Sherwood Forest taking from the rich and giving to the poor.

"We have a similar benefactor down here," he would say. "He is called "The King of Prussia."

Jan used to hang on his every word, listening with fascination to the tales of daring deeds and intrepid adventures that filled his young mind with wonder.

The King of Prussia's reputation had grown in leaps and bounds as he continued to ship cargoes of wine and fine silks into a small cove six miles south of Penzance. The Revenue men tried to catch him and it was often rumoured that they were perhaps, not quite as vigilant as they might be. There was not a single social gathering in the County that did not display the trappings of John Carter. Ladies dressed in fine satin sashes, men commenting slyly on the quality of the Brandy- the rewards of turning a blind eye to the goings-on at Prussia Cove.

Whilst Jan was ruminating over his new found knowledge, the girl returned with another jug of ale. John sat back in his chair and showed no signs of moving.

"What caused you to be confronted by those three ruffians in Penryn?" Jan asked.

"Do you know Lord Pendennis?"

"Know him?" Jan echoed. "I grew up with his son."

Jan recalled bitterly the childhood he had spent in Falmouth with Peter Pendennis. There was no love lost between the two. Pendennis had the inborn arrogance of the aristocracy and he didn't fail to show it. Jan, tinged with jealousy, had grown to hate the cocksure, conceited child, a hatred that often boiled over into violent displays of temper in the backyard of the small village school they both attended.

"I used to go school with him," Jan went on. "I have to confess he wasn't one of my greatest friends."

"It was him that set those rascals on me," John Carter replied.

"For what reason?"

"As you may know, I have a dubious reputation around these parts, mostly the result of hearsay and supposition. Well, it's true, I do run the odd cargo and it's true that goods often find their way into some of the finest houses in Cornwall. By doing this everyone is happy apart from the Revenue men. Lord Pendennis has benefited from my generosity on numerous occasions. In return he uses his considerable influence to ensure that the Customs men are suitably deployed when a run is in the offing. We have a very good working relationship and I have found him to be a most fair and reliable man."

Jan nodded his head in agreement although he remembered ruefully the whipping he received for stealing apples from his lordship's orchard.

"His son, however, is of a different character entirely as you already know. He has no regard for honour or trust and is only concerned with what he can make for himself. A short while ago I brought in a cargo from Bordeaux, in payment to Lord Pendennis I sent a crate of two dozen of the finest wines to be found in France together with a vat of the best French brandy."

John Carter paused and took a long swig from his mug.

"Unfortunately Lord Pendennis had been called up to London on business and the shipment was received by his son, Peter. It was obvious that he knew nothing of the dealings his father was undertaking. I learned later that Peter Pendennis flew into a rage and blamed all the ill-doings in the County on "The King of Prussia". Why he should become so angry, I do not know. Anyway, the upshot of it all was that he roused the Customs and Excise men into such a state of righteous indignation that they had no alternative but to search Prussia Cove."

John Carter tore off a piece of bread and dipped it in his ale.

"Of course," he continued, "they found nothing but caused a considerable amount of damage, just the same. I was getting a little tired of Master Pendennis- it was becoming difficult to remain a law-abiding citizen."

He winked at his companion and carried on.

"I decided to take him to court for the damage he did to my locks. On reflection it was a rash thing to do, there was no hope of a decision in my favour. The Revenue men were only doing their duty. However, the threat of court action seemed to have worked as I received a note from Pendennis apologising for his impulsive behaviour and would I care to collect a sum of two guineas from the gatehouse of Pendennis castle as a token of his regret.

I must admit that I was surprised by this uncharacteristic display of chivalry, As I was going to Falmouth on a small matter, I decided to call and collect the two guineas. I should have known better. The skirmish in which you fortunately intervened was the result of a well formulated plan to finish the King of Prussia off for good. The man in the gatehouse had orders to contact the three assailants the moment I called to collect the payment."

John Carter leant back and finished his drink. It was unusual for him to make such a long speech. The fact that he chose to say anything at all showed a respect for Jan that was not lost on the young man as he stirred the dying embers of the fire. He could imagine Peter Pendennis stooping to such a low level of trickery but he was surprised that he risked so much to settle what seemed, such a trivial matter. His father would never have resorted to such underhand tactics.

"Well lad, back to your problems- I promised that I would help you and that I shall do. How would you like to come and live with the King of Prussia for a while?"

Jan was fully aware of the implications of the offer but he was quick to answer. "If you've a mind to, it will be an honour to accept your invitation. I hope I can be of some use to you."

With that the two men shook hands and went out into the night. The owner of the Halfway House was waiting outside with two fresh horses. Bidding the fat Innkeeper a jovial farewell, they saddled up and trotted off.

The night had cleared. The stars shone brightly and the moon cast enough light to guide the sure-footed horses on the path to Prussia Cove.

Dawn was breaking as they approached the outskirts of Helston. The only thing to stir was a cat scurrying across their path as they clattered down the cobbled street of the old market town. At the bottom of the hill, the road offered two routes, one to Porthleven, the other to Breage and Penzance. They dismounted and led the horses up a steady incline towards the tiny village of Breage. The road was empty save for a horse and cart pulling a load of empty fish boxes bound for the fishing port of Porthleven. With a cheery greeting to the driver, John Carter remounted and led the way onto level ground. Jan rode alongside and allowed curiosity to get the better of him.

"Do you enjoy this kind of life?" he asked.

John Carter reflected on this for a moment, "Ay, I guess I do. There's more honest ways to make a living but none can offer the same excitement. I don't hold with taking from those who cannot afford it and those that can, will not miss a few guineas."

"But don't you ever worry about getting caught? It could be transportation or the gallows if you were."

"Every man has his time, Jan, call it fate. I care little for the risks of being caught. I have no wife or children to support."

With that he launched into an account of his childhood which kept Jan fascinated for the next hour.

John Carter was born in Cornwall in 1770. His parents had moved down from Shropshire three years earlier to eke out a precarious living from the land and sea. He had seven brothers and two sisters. Being the eldest, he had responsibility thrust upon him at an early age. It was while he was learning and displaying leadership skills that he earned the nickname, The King of Prussia. As a boy he had heard tales about the redoubtable Peter the Great, King of Prussia and he tried to model himself on the great leader, even changing the name of the cove where he lived from Porthleah to Prussia.

As he grew older, the knowledge he gained about the coastline and sea was second to none. It was even rumoured that the fishermen of Newlyn and Porthleven were moved to consult him when catches were poor. He became popular with all kinds of people, his easy manner and jovial wit winning over the most obstinate of men. He succeeded in breaking into the inner confines of Cornish society. This did not please his parents who had never entertained any airs above their station. But John Carter's greatest asset was his ability to understand and manipulate the minds of his fellow man. He knew the right pitch to adopt when he required a favour. It often caused petty jealousy amongst his brothers and sisters when they discovered the extent to which he was able to curry favour with his mother. The unpleasantness never lasted long with John's smooth talking and friendly smile winning the day.

When he was 18, it became apparent to his father that there was little chance of his eldest son continuing to work on the farm and he was forced to turn his attention to his second son, Henry, who displayed all the attributes of a well-to-do young man capable of maintaining the good name of the family. John disliked the pious attitude Henry showed but he was prepared to tolerate it for the sake of the family and happy that it left him to pursue his interests in other directions. He had heard from Newlyn that smuggling was a profitable business providing the right contacts were obtained in France. As he had no money his first task was to find a sponsor. This caused him a lot of anxiety as one word in the wrong circle could easily foil his plans before they begun.

After much thought, he kept coming back to one man. Cornwall was not well endowed with rich gentry so his choice was severely limited. Lord Godolphin was an old man. He had seen action all over the world in a brilliant military career which had resulted in him being awarded a seat in the House of Lords, a fat pension and a large mansion in Cornwall. At first he had taken an active part in the business of government, travelling to London twice a month to take his seat. As he got older, however, the journey became more tiresome and the dealings of Parliament, a bore. He stopped attending and life became exceedingly dull.

John Carter had met Lord Godolphin once. He had liked him from the start. Here was a man who shared his excitement for life. Although they only met briefly, John felt a mutual trust that went beyond the spoken word. How far that trust extended was a risk John Carter had to assess in his search for a sponsor.

After chewing over the idea he decided to approach the elderly gentleman. He was not sure how to bring up such a ticklish subject but his desire was strong and without giving it much thought, he found himself knocking on the door of Godolphin House.

After what seemed an eternity the door was opened by a courteous but suspicious butler. John stated his business and was shown into a drawing-room that adjoined the vast wood-panelled hallway. Although he was used to conversing with the gentry, he felt uncomfortable sitting on the edge of his chair in such grandiose surroundings. He had never been able to relax when faced with such opulence. He much preferred the snug of a small country Inn.

John still squirmed with embarrassment every time he related the tale. Sitting in Lord Godolphin's hall waiting for an audience was one of the longest moments in his life. Eventually the butler reappeared,

"Lord Godolphin will see you now," he announced stiffly unable to hide his distaste. He did not hold with his master encouraging the riff-raff of county.

John ignored him and strode across to the open door at the end of the hall. Sitting behind a large mahogany desk was a grey haired old man who, quill in hand, appearing to be writing profusely. As the young man stood tentatively on the threshold, he put the pen down and beckoned him in.

"Come in, come in. Don't stand there like a statue. Take a seat and tell me what you want."

Lord Godolphin's tone was brusque but not unkind. John did as he was told and sat down in the high-backed chair that was pulled up to the opposite side of the desk. He took a deep breath and said, "My name is John Carter and I come from Porthleah. It is a matter of business that brings me to your house."

He stopped, unsure how to continue.

"Go on, boy, I won't bite you."

"It is rather a delicate subject, sir. I find it difficult to know how to start."

"Try coming out with it straight- I don't like people who beat about the bush."

"I need a sponsor for a venture that, if successful, could bring a handsome return on the investment." John hesitated before adding lamely," I was wondering if you would be interested?"

At that first meeting the old man had looked him up and down, John recalling vividly the piercing blue eyes that gave nothing away.

"You will have to give me more information than that," he continued. "I want to know how much money is involved and to what purpose it will be used."

At that stage John Carter had been close to abandoning the whole scheme aware that he was putting his head in a noose if his assessment of Lord Godolphin's character proved false. However, having got this far he was not prepared to let the opportunity slip.

"Your outlay would initially be 200 guineas, enough for me to charter a boat and sail to France."

Lord Godolphin's face gave nothing away. At length, he answered slowly. "It is smuggling you want me to be a part of is it?"

"Trade,sir. Not smuggling."

"Pah! It's smuggling, such a trade is highly illegal, contrary to the laws of Government. I think, Mr.Carter you have made a grave error in coming here. I suggest you leave before you incriminate yourself even further."

Lord Godolphin stood up. "Wait, sir, please hear me out."

The steely blue eyes gave nothing away.

"I agree, smuggling is illegal but I can think of far greater injustices that go unpunished by the so-called government of this country. What about the people who are rotting in our prisons simply because they cannot afford to pay the taxes that are imposed upon them? What about the rich landowners who milk their employees dry and then refuse to spend money on them when they starve through the winter months? I have seen it happening right here in Cornwall, so if smuggling does happen to be against the law at least it will only affect those who can well afford the loss."

John sat back in his chair and let the anger subside. He was annoyed with himself for losing control. Lord Godolphin had sat down again and was impassively filling a clay pipe with tobacco.

"If it were not for the rich landowners," he replied slowly, "you or I would not be here today- we owe our existence, national status and stable government to them. Admittedly our maritime strength is important but for a country to be successful in the world it must manufacture and utilise its own resources."

"But surely the first priority of a country must be to its people, to see that they are fed and clothed. Not to a few rich souls who are able to prosper off the backs of the starving."

Lord Godolphin sighed. "This world is full of injustices. You have to grab opportunities when they present themselves."

"Therefore, sir, you do not condemn those less fortunate when they attempt to rectify some of the injustices?"

"If it is within the law- no. The plan you are asking me to be a party to, is not."

Lord Godolphin lit his pipe. He would have to be careful. This was a clever young man.

"Do I take it, sir, you are not prepared to consider a business transaction?"

The Lord's eyes flickered for a moment. Then he spoke sharply. "What kind of return would I get from the original investment?"

"I will repay the 200 guineas within a year plus a further 250. Also I will see that you are kept well supplied with the finest Brandy and Tobacco that France has to offer."

"Not a startling return for the risk involved."

"There will be no risk as far as you are concerned. Once I have chartered a boat there will be no way it can be associated with you. I will be the only person who knows and I give my word as a gentleman of honour that I will not reveal your involvement in the deal."

John, whose body had been taut throughout the interview, relaxed a fraction.

Lord Godolphin stared intently at the man in front of him. The idea of mellow Brandy and fine Tobacco did evoke a sneaking appeal and he had to admit to a grudging admiration for the effrontery of the boy who came straight out with such a daring proposition. But perhaps the most appealing factor was the excitement the deal offered. He had grown irritable of late, unable to grow old in a sedate and boring manner. He felt the familiar surge of excitement.

"I accept your proposition young man, although I cannot think for the life of me, why."

They shook hands and the deal was sealed. After a few minutes of idle chatter over a glass of mulled wine, John Carter left secure in the knowledge that a draft for 200 guineas had been made available to him at Tabb's bank in Penzance.

"And that was how it all began," said John after finishing his discourse. "So never give up hope, Jan, you never know what life might bring. If it hadn't been for Lord Godolphin I would still be dropping pots and shooting lines off St.Michael's Mount."

Jan grinned in the darkness wondering if he would ever have the effrontery to ask a perfect stranger for 200 guineas.

by John Platts

CHAPTER 3

The sun was well into the sky as the two horsemen approached the winding lane that led to Prussia Cove. Jan was desperately tired but his companion showed no signs of fatigue, not even the ugly gash on his forehead seemed to affect his wellbeing.

Dismounting and walking the horses down the narrow approach, Jan was struck by the natural beauty of the area. The clear blue sky afforded a magnificent view stretching across Mounts Bay from the small fishing village of Mousehole to the familiar outline of the Lizard peninsula in the far distance. The deep azure of the sea was in rich contrast to the stark, grey outcrops of granite that typified the rugged nature of the terrain. All around the hedgerows were alive with insects busy preparing for the onset of winter. Jan felt humbled, he had not given much thought to the land where he was born but this struck a cord. Here was a setting that was beyond his comprehension.

As the lane narrowed they had to proceed in single file. John went first, anxious that Jan should not take one of the side trails that could lead to him falling off the cliff. In fact the way was well grooved by many hoof-marks and wagon ruts, showing evidence of considerable activity over the last few weeks.

At the top of the inlet the descent divided into two, the one to the right led to Bessies Kindlywink, a popular drinking house and the one to the left led straight to the house of the King of Prussia. John led them forward but as soon as he stepped into the hallway of his stone built cottage he knew something was wrong. It was this uncanny sixth sense that had saved him on many occasions but this time he could not pinpoint the reason for his uneasiness. He did not have long to wait.

The kitchen door was flung open and a wizened old man with a slight stoop, burst through.

"They've bin master," he gasped with some agitation.

"Who's been?"

"The Revenue men. There were swarms of `em all over the place, they came in droves. I couldn't stop `em. All over the place." The old man was beside himself somehow feeling it was his fault that he hadn't been able to protect the home of his master.

"Calm yourself Jelbert, it wasn't your fault," John replied trying to assuage the old man's guilt.

Jan hovered by the door uncertain as to what to do next.

"Come into the parlour, both of you and let's get to the bottom of this, although I have my suspicions already."

John Carter led them into the parlour where the cinders of the previous night's fire had taken the chill off the darkened room. He bade both men to take a seat.

Jelbert's state of mind was not helped by the presence of a stranger whom he noticed for the first time.

John Carter sensed his uneasiness. "This is Jan Pendray, Jelbert, a good friend of mine who will be with us for a while. You may speak freely in front of him."

"I tried to stop `em," the old man wailed, "but what could I do? They charged all over the house like they were agents of the Devil."

"Did they search the outbuildings?"

"Aye, that they did master, took every last barrel of contraband with `em."

John's fist came crashing down on the wooden table in front of him with such force that Jan and the old man jumped off their seats. It was rare to see the King of Prussia give vent to his feelings with such an open display of anger. Jan noted the change in his new friend's face. The normally docile features had been replaced by an ashen mask of blind fury. In this state of mind he could see that the man was capable of doing anything.

And yet, the anger subsided as quickly as it arrived to be replaced by the twinkling eye and the hint of a smile playing around the corner of his mouth.

"Jelbert, make up a bed here for Jan then summon the men. I want a meeting at Bessies at 6 o'clock this evening." John Carter's voice was steady and confident, his momentary loss of control pushed far into the annals of his mind.

Jan was exhausted. The thought of a wash and a bed to lie on had been uppermost in his mind since leaving Breage village. Gratefully he followed Jelbert up the stairs and was shown into a modest sized room which overlooked Prussia Cove.

The old man pulled back the covers of the four poster bed and, after enquiring whether his services were required any further, he departed to leave Jan to his own devices. He gazed out of the window contemplating his immediate future.

He knew he was entering the services of a very dangerous man who could well lead him on a path that travelled on the wrong side of the law. It was the thought of the alternatives that cast away any lingering doubts. He had thrown his lot in with the King of Prussia and to hell with the consequences.

Jan awoke at four o'clock, the atmosphere was warm and humid in the bedroom. Outside there was a stillness that hinted of an approaching thunderstorm. He got out of bed feeling refreshed. His body ached from the previous night's exertions but overall he could not complain. His clothes had been laid out neatly across the back of a chair and a jug of fresh water had been placed next to the washbasin. After soaking his face he felt ready to face the world. Downstairs the first person he bumped into was John Carter. It was evident that he had not been to bed, his eyelids were hanging heavily above his eyes and the cut on his forehead was starting to blacken with rancid blood.

"Did you sleep well, Jan?" It was a statement rather than a question as his mind had already moved on to other things. "I would like you to attend the meeting at Bessies tonight. I will introduce you to some of the men. It will show that you are one of us."

John nodded his assent and the King of Prussia disappeared into one of the rooms that led off the narrow hallway. He had an hour to kill before the meeting so he decided to explore the cove. The cottage stood on a pinnacle commanding an excellent view of the rocky inlet known as Prussia Cove. At first, he was surprised how small the area was, he had imagined the cove to be at least as big as the harbour at Porthleven but there were only two small inlets capable of taking a medium sized fishing boat. Despite this, the advantages were obvious. The only access was by a tiny pathway to the south and a narrow cart track to the north. The rest of the area was a mass of brambles, thickets and gorse, from above it was practically impossible to see into the cove.

Jan approached the beach from the north side, walking down a manufactured track which was evidently well used. Across the first beach a wooden bridge had been constructed to aid the horses in their struggle to the top of the cliff. In the rocks, narrow grooves had been chiselled out which allowed the carts to be dragged right to the water's edge. The inlet was no more than fifteen feet across but at high tide it was possible to imagine a depth of twenty feet. A fully laden fishing smack could creep into the inlet without being spotted from above or from the prying eyes of the Revenue spyglasses over in Penzance harbour.

Jan stood on the quayside watching four or five boats ride gently on their moorings trying to imagine what it would be like to cross to France in, what appeared to be, nothing more than a cork. He was beginning to develop a secret admiration for the men who risked their lives with such a dubious occupation.

Looking up at the hanging greenery as it disturbed the flow of cascading water sending out clouds of translucent spray, he could see the enchantment of this piece of Cornish coast. He easily imagined John Carter as a child, playing hide and seek in the numerous rock pools and searching for crabs under the sea washed stones that littered the foreshore.

On the opposite side of the quay a narrow path wound itself up the side of the cliff to a couple of thatched cottages which Jan took to be fishermen's huts. The path continued upwards until it disappeared in a confusion of greenery at the top of the cliff. It wasn't difficult to see that one man, stationed by the cottages, could give a twenty minute warning to those working below.

Jan crossed to the other side of the harbour by means of a rope walkway and strolled up the slipway, past the winch used to bring boats above the waterline, until he was standing in front of the thatched cottages. They had no windows and the doors were locked.

"A few secrets here," he thought as he stood looking at the sturdy, granite walls. His ruminating was cut short by the sound of a footstep behind. A man stood next to him.

Where he came from, Jan had no idea but he was painfully aware that the stranger was eyeing him with a good deal of suspicion. He bore the features of a typical Cornish fisherman. His face carried the weatherbeaten expression of someone who had spent a large part of his life at sea.

The grudging stare, the suspicion of strangers, Jan knew well but there was more than that in the man's eyes. Was it fear? Guilt? Or maybe a conscience, Jan was unable to fathom.

"You've no business poking your nose around here," said the stranger. His voice did not match his features. He spoke with a cultured air, hinting of an education.

"Where are you from?" The stranger barked the question with such force that Jan jumped.

"I'm staying with John Carter," he stuttered in reply.

The man eyed him curiously, surprise etched in his expression.

"Many are they who have interwoven their fate with the King of Prussia, none have cause to thank him. The Lord is the only saviour for those who choose a path of licentiousness and debauchery."

Jan winced, he always mistrusted religious fanatics. Their convictions seemed to smack of hypocrisy. He did not like this man.

"Mark my words, the ways of the Almighty should not be treated with derision lest you be cast into the inferno of eternal damnation."

The stranger reminded him of Charles Wesley whom he had heard preach in the market place in Falmouth. The only difference was that Wesley's oration carried a complete devotion to the Methodist cause. With this man there did not appear to be the same conviction.

The stranger moved on up the cliff path still muttering about the wickedness of mankind and the path to reconciliation in the eyes of the Lord.

Jan sat down and looked out to sea. It was the first time he had a chance to take stock of the events that had happened with bewildering speed. On many occasions during the last twenty four hours he had tried to eradicate the image of Anna from his mind but each time it came thundering back with all the intensity of the sea crashing onto the North Cornish coast. His love, he felt sure, would never die but he could not expect Anna to feel the same. She was growing into a very beautiful woman and would soon experience the compliments paid to her by all the fine gentlemen in the county. For the sake of a pledge from a mere boy, she would not be able to resist the temptations that would surely be placed in front of her. She had always been headstrong and impulsive – never predictable.

Jan sighed in resignation as he watched the sallow sea gently wash onto the shingle beach. He knew in his heart that the love he felt could never bear fruit, it was an impossible dream and the sooner he banished it from his mind, the sooner he could contemplate the future.

The day was fast receding as he climbed back up the cliff to the house. Rainclouds were scudding across the distant horizon causing a premature greyness that ushered in the night across Mounts Bay.

While Jan was out, John Carter had slept. He felt refreshed and confident. His mind was clear and he had already formulated a plan to avenge his loss. He was aware of the risk of pursuing the matter further but, as so many people in the vicinity had benefited from his illicit trade, he was fairly confident that there would be few repercussions. He had made sure that many in positions of authority had been ensnared. However, it was pride that dictated his proposed plan, it was up to him to persuade the rest of the men that it could be achieved without further disruption.

Jan and John Carter walked up the hill to Bessies together. It was the only drinking place for eight miles but the clientele consisted mainly of fishermen and the odd farm hand. It was rare for strangers to cross the threshold. As they approached the Inn an enormous woman filled the open door, it didn't take Jan long to realise that she was Bessie.

"Welcome home, Cap'n," she boomed in a voice that shook the foundations of the house. "They all be waiting for 'ee in the parlour."

"Thanks, Bessie, it's good to be back," he replied giving her an enormous slap on the backside. Jan slid past the laughing woman hoping she would not exact her revenge on him.

It was dim inside the parlour. John motioned Jan to a vacant chair and sat down at the head of a long oak table. As his eyes became accustomed to the light he was aware of a dozen staring faces. He met each man's scrutiny with a confidence he did not feel but he only flinched once when he recognised the man he had encountered on the cliff.

"So much for your pious ideas," he thought to himself.

The twelve men in the room covered the whole spectrum of society in the County bound together only by the illicit trade with France.

Sensing the growing suspicion John stood up to speak.

"Let me introduce a friend of mine," he announced to the assembly. "Jan Pendray from Falmouth, he saved my life."

No more was said, such was the charisma of the King of Prussia. John Carter surveyed the group carefully. He knew he had a difficult job to persuade them to follow his plan of action.

"As you know, the Revenue men came and confiscated all the goods we had brought in from Brittany on the last run. Why they came I don't know but I have my suspicions. What I propose gentlemen, is that we reclaim what is rightfully ours from the Custom House on Penzance Quay."

The men were silent for a moment then everyone started talking at once.

"What about the Guards?" asked one man.

"It's too risky," said another. "They'll not leave us be if we go that far."

A man with well-cut breeches which distinguished him from the others said, " I stand to lose a lot of money if we don't get the cargo back."

John let them continue for a while then, with a loud cough, he called the meeting to order.

"I know it is a risky operation but if it succeeds and we get rid of the shipment quickly, there is no way they can prove who is responsible. The vital thing is that no one gets caught and no one is found with contraband on their person."

He stopped for a moment observing the reactions of his men. There was silence, each man chewing over the proposals that John Carter had put to them. None of them were cowards they had all proved themselves to be worthy followers of the King of Prussia, but this was different. Their leader was asking them to risk far more than they had ever done before. Any slip and it would be transportation at the very least. At worst it could mean the rope.

"I only want committed men for this venture," John continued. "If you feel the risk is too great then you are free to go. I know a number of you have families to consider."

Still no one spoke. The atmosphere in the cramped parlour was tense.

"Those in favour raise your right hand."

Jan and John Carter raised their hands simultaneously. The rest hesitated. One by one, six men got up from the table and made for the door.

"I've got a baby six weeks old to think about," said one

"I've got a wife who's proper poorly with sleeping sickness," said another.

The man Jan had met on the cliff spat on the floor in front of the passing men muttering about divine guidance and loyalty to the cause. Excluding Jan and John, there were six men left in the room.

"I want no recriminations on those who have left," snapped John an edge of authority creeping into his voice. " This is a dangerous operation. I want men who can be trusted and will not lose their nerve when the going gets tough. Those who have left, have others to worry about, we have little to worry about apart from ourselves."

The man who spat on the floor maintained a surly silence.

"Jan, let me introduce you to the men."

He started from the right of the table with Tegron Smith, a mealy-mouthed man with a large scar across his forehead, He nodded in acknowledgement without speaking. Next to him sat Jerome Bartha, a fisherman from Newlyn. His windswept face and ruddy complexion cast an eerie glow when he lent close to the burning candle placed in the centre of the table. Completing that side of the table sat Jake Tanna a huge man with fists like granite. John introduced him as a miner from South Crofty and it was easy to see why. Dust had eaten into his skin leaving pallid blotches over his face.

"No wonder he stayed," thought Jan as he pictured the giant man slaving away a thousand feet below, ten hours a day all for a mere pittance.

Opposite Jake sat Ben Rescorla, a weasel-faced man whom John described as the only man capable of scaling the North wall of St. Michaels Mount without a rope. Judging by the lithe movements of his hands Jan did not doubt it for one moment.

In the middle sat Daniel Pentecost, the man who had exuded an air of refinement earlier.

"An honour to make your acquaintance, Mr. Pendray." He stood up and offered Jan his hand.

"A man of breeding," thought Jan, as he willingly returned the handshake.

Finally he came the Bible puncher.

"And last of all, I would like you to meet Henry Carter, my brother."

Jan's mouth fell open with astonishment. He had never expected the man to be related to the King of Prussia.

A ghost of a smile crossed Henry Carter's face. "We have met. I tried to warn him off associating with such a motley crew."

The men around the table laughed. Evidently they took his holy pronouncements with a pinch of salt. Jan smiled with them, confident that such able and daring men would not take the risk of working with a man they did not trust.

"I cannot think of a group of men I would rather serve with," said Jan with a sincerity that had the assembled group nodding their approval.

"And now down to business." The briskness of John Carter's tone indicated the end of formalities. For two hours the eight men discussed the plan of campaign until everyone was fully conversant with their part in the action. Finally John stood up and addressed the group.

"You now have two hours to prepare. We will meet back here at one o'clock and remember, I want no bloodshed- killing will destroy the goodwill we have built up throughout the County."

With his final words ringing in their ears, the men made their way out of the smoke-filled room leaving behind Jan, the King of Prussia and his brother. The candle had burnt low casting eerie shadows across their faces. Jan's curiosity got the better of him and he turned to Henry Carter and said, "how does a man of the cloth get mixed up with a gang of smugglers?"

Henry stared at the young man in front of him his piercing eyes penetrating the dark like beams of luminous light.

"The Lord moves in mysterious ways. My calling refuses to accept the fact the rich should get richer while the poor live in poverty and ill health. If I can do something to right the injustices of this country it goes a long way towards absolving my conscience. Last week I preached to the miners of Bissoe at Gwennap Pit – half were on the point of starvation."

His voice shook with emotion. "I could see women with shawls over their shoulders to cover the grotesque pock-marked skin, I could see young children little more than babies bearing the black marks of pit dust and worst of all, I could see the expressions on the faces of their menfolk. Despair issued from every pore as they saw the hopeless task of providing for their loved ones. However hard they worked, they were at the mercy of the pit owners who can choose whether they live or die. That's why I engage in illicit trade, Jan Pendray."

Jan felt uncomfortable. He got the impression that Henry Carter was blaming him for the miners' fate. He was vaguely aware of the poverty that had descended on the mining population. His father had often talked about it. As a young boy it had set his mind to wondering why some well-dressed ladies could drive around Falmouth's Castle Drive whilst others had to walk. Once he had tried to jump on the back of a carriage but was brushed away, unable to understand. Now he had grown to accept the divisions of society although he still found it difficult to stomach the arrogance the gentry seemed to possess when it came to dealing with lower classes.

"I agree with you Mr. Carter, there are those who need more, but smuggling is against the law and carries a heavy sentence for those who get caught."

"There are degrees of illegality, Jan Pendray, just as there are different standards in the pursuit of the gospel. I do not regard smuggling as a serious crime as it does no harm to anyone and much good for those who can benefit from a little charity now and then."

Jan let the matter rest. He was not convinced that Henry Carter had the well-being of his fellow men at heart.

CHAPTER 4

Jan and the King of Prussia were stationed outside Bessies in plenty of time to greet the first arrivals. The evening was dark although the rain had stopped for the moment. Conditions were ideal for the assault on the warehouse.

John Carter had taken a calculated risk that the contraband was still in Penzance. It was likely that it had been taken to the warehouse on Custom House Quay. It was not easy to conceal seven kegs of brandy, twenty-four large vats of wine and two packages of tobacco, so it was a logical guess that the Revenue would keep it on their premises for the time being. He knew that speed was of the essence if the plan was to be successful. Surprise would be his biggest weapon as the Excise men would not expect such a rapid response.

Jake Tanna was the first to arrive, his huge frame leaning forward as he tugged the reins of six pack mules. They would carry the load once it had been snatched back to its rightful owners. The others began appearing from different directions until, at ten minutes past one, all were assembled and ready for the task ahead.

The column wound its way up from Prussia Cove their horses fresh and lively in the cool night air. Each man passed the time by going over their appointed task aware that any slip up could prove fatal to the success of the expedition. When they reached Marazion, John Carter led them onto the sandy beach to eradicate the noise that the horses would have made on the cobbled approach to Penzance. From then on no one spoke.

Jan could feel the tension mounting, he felt good. He had never experienced such excitement and his body buzzed with anticipation.

The Harbour at Penzance sticks out into Mounts Bay like a sore thumb giving protection to the boats within. On this occasion the only boat docked was the old lugger that plied forth between the Isles of Scilly and the mainland. The fishing fleet was safely ensconced in Newlyn harbour a mile to the West. John Carter smiled with satisfaction as his keen eyes spotted the mast of the lugger as it speared upwards into the murky sky.

"Good, the less people the better."

To gain access to the warehouse from the beach was impossible without returning to the road. John had considered the possibility of a snatch from the sea but rejected it on the grounds that it would take too long to load a boat and also the added danger of being caught in possession by the powerful Revenue cutter should things go wrong.

The riders dismounted and handed the reins to Tegron Smith, he was to remain on the beach with the horses. The six mules, Jake Penna led further up the beach where he deftly tied rabbit skins around each hoof to muffle the sound when they returned to the cobbled road. The rest of the men followed John Carter back to the road. From now on silence was vital. In single file the band of men moved stealthily through the old part of town. At the Causeway Inn, Jerome Bartha stopped. His job was to ensure that the route back to the horses was safe. Jan watched him melt silently into the darkness. The rest carried on until they reached the edge of the harbour. It was high tide, the water lapped over harbour wall and spilled onto the cobbled wharf. Empty crab pots slew about as the rivulets of water found their way back into the harbour. Here another look-out was posted as it commanded an excellent view of the inner harbour.

The tension clawed at the stomachs' of the men. Jan could feel vibrations of excitement coursing through his veins, only John Carter appeared to be at ease.

"The stuff should be over there," he whispered, pointing to a large granite building that stood isolated from the Custom House. Jan could see that it was not an easy place to raid, surrounded on three sides by water the only access was past the Custom House itself. An oil lamp burned in a downstairs room. When anything of importance was in the warehouse the Revenue always posted a twenty-four hour watch. John had reckoned on there being no more than three men on duty.

On the right hand side of the harbour the road led off to Newlyn. It was used frequently linking the two harbours. Consequently a number of wooden huts had been constructed by the roadside so that the business and tally men could work on transactions without having to walk up the hill to Market Jew Street. Daniel Pentecost surveyed the huts casually. He knew which one he wanted without much more than a cursory glance. He chose the one that was slightly away from the others with a granite wall built around it.

"Ideal," he murmured and set about his allotted task.

Meanwhile the rest remained in the shadows outside the Customs house, Jake making a valiant effort to restrain the mules that were getting fretful at the smell of rotting fish. At 2.45, a broad streak of flame leapt up from the west side of the harbour. Daniel Pentecost had done his task well. The hut was ablaze within minutes. Even the dampness from the previous night's rain could not hold back the fierce heat as the flames caught hold.

The four figures remained motionless in the shadows. Suddenly the silence was broken by the sound of running feet. A man appeared through the gloom and hammered on the door of the Customs house.

"One of the huts is on fire, come quickly," he shouted to the emerging guards. The three men inside grabbed their coats and ran towards the blazing huts. Daniel Pentecost re-joined the others and they all sprinted in the direction of the warehouse with Jake Tanna desperately trying to pull the mules into a trot. Once at the warehouse, Jan could see no possible means of entry, there were no windows on the ground floor and a vast impregnable iron door. He had not reckoned with the talents of Ben Rescorla. Instantly the little man set about climbing the granite wall. It was sheer poetry to watch his lithe movements as he scaled the vertical wall like a cat. Once on the roof the rest was easy, a half-open skylight and he disappeared from view. In a matter of seconds he had opened the big iron door.

"It's all here, Cap'n, stacked as neat as you like over there." Ben led them to the stash of contraband.

Speed was now of the essence, they had to get the goods loaded and away before the guards came back. Stumbling around in the dark, the men loaded the mules as quickly as they could. It took ten minutes before the final consignment was safely aboard the last pack mule. Casting a last glance around the store, John Carter hurried out into the night. Jake was fighting manfully with the mules as they moved painfully slowly away from the building. The flames of the fire had died back. Soon the guards would be back.

John Carter joined in the cursing of the mules as the men forced the reluctant animals along the quay.

As the first mule drew level with Customs house the sound of footsteps could clearly be heard from the direction of the fire. It would be a matter of minutes before the guards saw what was happening. Henry Carter detached himself from the convoy and moved quickly towards the ringing footsteps, his moccasin sandals making no sound on the hard cobble stones.

A shout followed by a long groan indicated that Henry Carter had laid into the three guards. It gave the mules a precious few seconds to pass the Customs House and off the quay.

Now all hell broke loose around the harbour. The commotion Henry had started attracted others. Lights went on in the cabin of the Isles of Scilly lugger and men started to appear at doorways still drowsy with sleep. One of the Excise men started shouting.

"Stop those men in the name of the law." He was pointing in the vague direction of the town but the darkness made him unsure as to where they were.

Jerome Bartha, the lookout posted on the harbour, was waiting by the winch chain as the mules moved slowly away from the quay. He pitched in with the others and cajoled the reluctant beasts along the road.

John Carter did not relax. They were not out of danger yet. The local militia was stationed at the bottom of Market Jew Street, only a hundred yards from the Causeway Inn where Jerome Bartha was waiting. John knew the commotion issuing from the harbour was bound to arouse their attention. They had to reach Tegron Smith and the horses if they were to make a clear get away.

Of Henry Carter and Daniel Pentecost nothing was heard. John did not worry. They both knew that once the task had been undertaken, personal safety was their own concern. His main task was to see that the contraband was safely distributed before the Militia caught up with them.

The first signs of dawn were creeping over the skyline as the King of Prussia led his men down onto the slipway that led to the beach. Tegron Smith was waiting anxiously with the horses.

"You've certainly started something over there Cap'n," he said looking at the plume of smoke rise above the harbour.

"So far, so good, Tegron but we're not out of the woods yet. The Militia will be on to us shortly. Leave Henry's and Daniel's horses tethered here. The rest of you-split."

He did not need to speak twice, the men took a mule each and set off in different directions.

Jan and John remained in the lee of the slipway.

"We'll stay here for a while, Jan, just in case the Militia happen this way."

John Carter began to breathe easier, a glow of satisfaction radiating from his face. The operation had gone without a hitch. His only lingering doubt was the extent his brother had gone to in order to delay the Excise guards.

The last mule had all but disappeared when the clatter of hooves could be heard coming from Penzance. The two men were instantly alert. The horses were approaching rapidly in their direction.

John's face broke into a manic smile. "Come on, Jan. We'll lead these militiamen a right dance before we're through."

He was quickly astride his horse with Jan only a second behind. The day was dawning rapidly so the two riders had little protection apart from the avenue of trees that led to the tiny village of Crowlas. The horses dashed up the slipway, across the Marazion road and took the fork to the right. Just as they reached the avenue of trees a group of seven horsemen rounded the bend and caught sight of the two smugglers. With a yell of triumph they galloped off in hot pursuit.

The road through Crowlas led over the downs and on towards the fishing port of St. Ives. Once out of the village there was little protection available to the fugitives. Jan cast an eye over his shoulder and could see that the militiamen were no more than a hundred yards behind. Another mile and they would be within musket range.

John had also realised the danger. Picking his route carefully he guided them off the road and down towards a group of trees that lay to his right. Jan let his horse choose the way and the sure-footed steed negotiated the granite outcrops with ease. The militia quickly saw what had happened and split into two groups, one maintaining the chase, the other circulating to cut off the entry to the wood. It was going to be a close run thing as the two men galloped across an open meadow that lay before the trees. A musket shot rang out. Jan heard the lead bullet whine over his head and saw it ricochet off a rock ten feet away. Another crack! This time the bullet kicked up dirt in front of John's horse but still they rode on. They gained the woods with twenty yards to spare.

"We'll have to ditch the horses and make a run for it."

Throwing the reins away they jumped into the dense undergrowth. Jan stumbled on blindly, his lungs gasping for air as the chase began to take its toll. He fixed his eyes firmly on the figure in front and refused to let his legs give way. He was frightened now there seemed no way even the King of Prussia could get them out of this predicament. The militiamen had the wood surrounded it was only a matter of time. John ploughed on relentlessly every few seconds gasping words of encouragement to the ailing Jan. They could hear the voices of their pursuers quite clearly now, the noose was tightening around their necks. A shot rang out from amidst the trees and a scream was heard to their left.

John laughed harshly. "The silly fools are firing at themselves! Keep going Jan we'll beat them yet."

Barely conscious Jan stumbled on, his legs acting on impulse rather than design. He was driven on by the strongest of all man's instincts- fear. Without realising it Jan crashed out of the woods and seemed to be running on grass, the going was easier but his tortured body was almost beyond recall. He staggered on his eyes fixed doggedly on the man in front. They plunged into a confusion of outhouses. Where they were, Jan had no idea, he didn't really care he just wanted to stop running. John Carter was well aware of where they were. He knew he was taking a huge risk but there was no alternative. He had led Jan into the grounds of Godolphin House.

By entering the woods they had gained precious seconds but it would not be long before the Militiamen regained the scent. The two fugitives pressed on to the main house and fell against the huge oak door. John managed to find enough strength to pull the cord. A jangling sound echoed from somewhere in the house.

They waited in tense silence their freedom hanging on a knife edge. After what seems a lifetime, the door opened. It was the butler who had shown such a distaste for John Carter the last time he had crossed the threshold. Without waiting for an invitation John pushed past him and led Jan inside. The door slammed shut before the startled butler could demand an explanation. He recovered quickly.

"What is the meaning of this?" He bellowed, his voice unable to disguise the contempt he felt for the two vagabonds who had arrived covered in mud and sweat, on his master's doorstep.

"Get me your master, quickly- it is a matter of life and death." John Carter pleaded.

The urgency of his request and the state of their appearance made the butler hesitate. It was only the fact that he had seen his master engaged in conversation with the man before him that stopped himself from summoning assistance and having the two dishevelled creatures thrown off the estate.

"The master is still in bed, he won't take too kindly to being woken at this hour."

The sound of horses on the drive outside could be clearly heard, causing the butler to reach for the door. Fortunately, at this point, Lord Godolphin appeared at the top of the stairs clad in his nightgown.

"Trehorne, what is going on?" He demanded, not at first seeing the two men.

John Carter aware of the urgency of the situation called up the stairs.

"We need your help, sir, desperately. There is a party of Militiamen outside your door and they are screaming for our blood. Our only chance is to trust to your kindness and hope you will not reveal our presence here."

Lord Godolphin descended the stairs slowly.

"So, it is John Carter again. Our paths often cross but we rarely seem to meet."

"I wish it could be under more pleasant circumstances my Lord but on this occasion it is not to be."

There was a loud hammering on the door.

"Open up in the name of the law," a voice bellowed from outside.

Lord Godolphin was quick to sum up the situation. "Quick! this way, both of you."

He ushered the two men into a small room off the hallway.

"Leave this to me, Trehorne."

Jan and John Carter slipped gratefully into their allotted hiding place.

They heard the butler open the door and listened intently.

"We have reason to believe that two men are hiding on your premises, one of whom bears a resemblance to John Carter better known as the King of Prussia." The man who had issued the statement bore the stripes of a Sergeant in the Militia.

Trethorne stood uncomfortably by the door unsure what to say. The Sergeant continued.

"We need permission from Lord Godolphin to search the grounds."

At this moment Lord Godolphin revealed himself to the officer.

"What's the trouble, Sergeant?"

Seeing Lord Godolphin in his sleeping attire took the Sergeant by surprise. He coughed and his confident manner dissipated.

"We would like your permission to search the house and grounds your Lordship," the Sergeant stammered, with a respect that was not present in his voice when he spoke to the butler.

"And for what reason?" queried Lord Godolphin.

"We have been chasing two men across the downs from Penzance. They were last seen running across your lawns in the direction of the house."

"And what, pray, prompted these two men to enter my grounds at such an ungodly hour?"

"Last night a Counting House was set on fire in Penzance harbour. It was a decoy to lure the harbour guards away from the quay, thus enabling a group of men to steal a quantity of confiscated goods from the warehouse. We were alerted by the guards and were fortunate enough to intercept two men as they made their getaway. I am certain that one of them was the King of Prussia. Now, if you please, may we have your permission to continue the search?"

The Sergeant was becoming impatient. Unless he continued the search immediately he could see them slipping from his grasp.

Lord Godolphin paused for a moment, staring intently at the Sergeant.

Sergeant Crowlas was not at his best when dealing with the aristocracy. His upbringing had been simple and humble. He had been brought up to know his place and respect his betters. His strongest asset was his determination to do well in the militia. If he could capture the King of Prussia it would do his career no harm at all.

Lord Godolphin with the benefit of years, read this on the face of the young Sergeant.

"I will allow you to search the grounds but not the house," he said abruptly. "No one has been inside this house today. If they had I would have known about it."

Sergeant Crowlas hesitated, he would have liked to search the house just to make sure but he had to remember he was dealing with a member of the aristocracy.

"Well, if I have your word Lord Godolphin I can but say thank you for allowing us your time and I hope we can catch this pair of murderers."

With that the Sergeant spun on his heel and started detailing his men to search the grounds.

"Wait, Sergeant, did you say murderers?"

"Aye,that I did, Sir. One of the guards was knocked unconscious whilst trying to protect the warehouse- he is in a bad way."

Lord Godolphin closed the door his face clouded with anger. He marched quickly across the hallway and into the room where John and Jan sat peeping through the closed curtains.

John started to speak but was cut short by Lord Godolphin.

"Murderers! I will not be a party to murder."

He was incandescent with fury, his frail body shaking with rage.

John stood back with astonishment. "What murder? We have not committed murder."

He was genuinely mystified and not a little alarmed. One word from Lord Godolphin and the militia would be in straight away.

"The Sergeant says that one of the Customs guards on the quay was knocked unconscious and you say you have nothing to do with it?"

Lord Godolphin's voice cut through the atmosphere like a knife. Realisation began to dawn on the King of Prussia. Silently he cursed the stupidity of his pious brother. Aloud he said, "I know nothing of this, I swear it, neither does Jan here. You have my word on it."

"Do you expect me to believe that? You planned the whole foolish operation just to satisfy your own pride. Well you have gone too far this time John Carter. Trehorne fetch the militia."

"No, wait. When we first met I gave you a pledge that I was a gentleman of honour. I have never given you a cause to doubt that so I say again, as a gentleman of honour, we had nothing to do with the condition of the Customs guard."

The features of the old man softened a little but he was still angry. Why did this young pup have to get mixed up in such a serious accusation?

"I grant you that I have never doubted you word in the past," Lord Godolphin said gruffly, but I am not prepared to accept that you had nothing to do with the incident."

"Will it pacify you if I give you this undertaking? I swear as a gentleman that the man responsible will be brought to justice."

Jan gasped. If the man had died then he would have to betray his own brother.

The old man's voice returned to normal. "That seems reasonable but I will not easily forgive what you have inflicted upon me this morning."

With that, Lord Godolphin let the matter rest. He walked over to the mahogany cabinet standing in the corner of the room and produced a bottle of Mead and three glasses. They drank in silence, the atmosphere still not restored to normal. Jan was on the point of exhaustion. His body was trembling and his mind confused by the dramatic turn of events. Ten minutes ago he thought he was on the way to prison. Somehow the King of Prussia had saved their skins.

Where he went now he did not know, everything had been going so well. Once again he had cast his fate into the hands of a smuggler of dubious reputation. His tired musings were cut short by Lord Godolphin who, having watched the militia depart down the drive, signalled the two men to leave.

John Carter shook the old man's hand and said, "I cannot thank you enough my Lord, you have put yourself at risk by offering us sanctuary. I only hope I will be able to repay your kindness in the future."

Lord Godolphin grunted muttering something inaudible in reply. They were led through the kitchen and out through a side door into a walled garden with a gate at the far end.

"God go with you John Carter and with your friend. I have not got it in my heart to be angry with you for long." Lord Godolphin smiled and waved them to the gate that spelt freedom. He watched them go, a faint smile playing around his lips. "There but for the grace of God," he thought before shutting the gate and returning to the sleep from which he was so rudely interrupted.

CHAPTER 5

an and John were greatly relieved to be out of danger, at least, for the time being. The night's adventure had taken its toll on Jan who was feeling desperately tired and more than a little apprehensive as to the outcome of the raid. The idea, which in the beginning was little more than a schoolboy prank, had escalated into something far more serious. If the guard died, the whole might of the Militia would descend on Prussia Cove and the surrounding area.

John Carter shared Jan's feelings. Inwardly he was cursing the stupidity of his brother. There had been no need for it. Had he not issued a warning beforehand that any violence would destroy the goodwill they enjoyed in the community? It had been his own flesh and blood who had disobeyed his instruction. To make matters worse he had pledged his word to Lord Godolphin that he would bring the culprits to justice should the man die.

Jan could see the heavy burden his friend was carrying. In the short time he had known him he had not seen him in such low spirits. Taking the initiative, Jan steered them both in the general direction of Prussia Cove. They walked in silence not noticing the watery sunrise as it rose majestically over a calm sea. As they approached the hamlet of Trescowe John Carter had recovered a little and led his companion down a lane to the right, which took them past a disused mill and down to the Hayle River. Nestled into the bank, stood a small mud hut.

"It's too dangerous to go back to Prussia Cove, Jan. We'll hole up here for a while until I can find out exactly what is going on."

Jan was grateful to hear the edge of confidence returning to his friend's voice. Jan nodded his agreement and followed him inside. The hut was little more than a small room. It had evidently been used for storing contraband in the past. It had no windows and smelt of stale wine, mingling with the sickly sweet odour of stale tobacco. In the corner was a pile of dry sacks. The two men slumped thankfully onto their makeshift bed and were immediately asleep.

It was evening when Jan awoke, the setting sun visible through the cracks around the door. He got up slowly taking care not to disturb the prone figure next to him. He wandered down to the river's edge and plunged his head into the cool, clear water. The first shock of cold water took his breath away but he stood up feeling refreshed. He suddenly realised he was hungry. Glancing back to the hut he saw no sign of movement from John so he made his way back up the path to Trescowe. The first house he came to had a thatched roof, supplemented by large slabs of mud where the straw ran thin. It gave the impression of an old dwelling built by wattle and daub in the Middle Ages. Surveying the building for a moment Jan decided to knock on the door. After a long delay in which nothing happened, Jan decided to move on. However, just as he was about to leave, the door opened a fraction and an old woman poked her head out.

"What do 'ee want?" She croaked. "I don't want no fish, no nuthin."

She was about to slam the door in Jan's face but he managed to speak. "I just want to purchase a bite to eat for myself and my friend. I can pay you."

Jan produced a shilling piece and let the sun glint on its shiny surface. The old woman gazed at him suspiciously.

"I ain't got no food, it's all I can do to feed meself, let alone provide for the likes of 'ee."

"Just some bread and a lump of cheese would be enough. I'm sure the King of Prussia would be most grateful."

At this remark she opened the door a fraction more and looked Jan up and down.

"Don't look much of a smuggler to me, too young by far."

"I can assure you I am a friend of the King of Prussia."

The old woman stared at him, the lines on her forehead narrowed to a wizened frown.

"A shillin, did you say? Can't buy much with that these days." She turned and went inside closing the door behind her.

Jan stood uncertainly wondering whether she would come out again. Eventually the door opened and a scaly hand thrust a package towards him. He pressed the shilling into the old woman's hand and the door snapped shut.

Jan walked slowly back to the hut, unwrapping the parcel as he went. Inside were four huge chunks of bread, a piece of cheese and two large cuts of cooked ham— a veritable feast for a starving man.

"All I can do to feed meself," Jan mimicked with a grin.

John was awake when he got back. He looked refreshed and pounced on the parcel of food with obvious delight.

"Where did you get this?" He enquired incredulously.

"From an old lady in Trescowe, who was willing to part with some sustenance on hearing the words, King of Prussia."

"That must have been Ma Shaw – dear old soul. She doesn't like strangers. Seventy-six she is and still walks into Penzance on market days. I'll see she gets an extra ration the next time we call."

"Is there going to be a next time?" Jan asked as they munched hungrily.

John's eyes narrowed for a second.

"I hope so, Jan, I really do but at the moment our fate is in the lap of the Gods."

"What are we going to do about it?"

"First of all, I'm going to make a trip into Penzance and see if I can discover what happened to the man my stupid brother so foolishly attacked."

"That's utter madness," Jan cried. "The whole town will be swarming with Militia. They are bound to recognise you."

"That's a risk I have to take, I must find out the true extent of his injuries. If they are serious I shall never be able to return to Prussia Cove again."

"It's still madness," Jan retorted. "I've a better idea, why don't you let me go. I'm not known in Penzance and there is no reason for anyone to associate me with Prussia Cove."

"What about the Militia? They chased you out of town, remember?"

""I'm sure they didn't get a good look at my face and even so, it is far less of a risk for me to go than you."

John Carter looked at his young companion. He could see the keenness burning in his eyes. He knew in his heart that it was foolish to consider going but was it fair to entrust such a delicate task to a mere boy? But he had to know what was going on. John sat in silence weighing up the situation. Finally he said, "O.K. you can go but you understand that all I want is information about the guard. You are not to take any risks."

Jan nodded his head vigorously, delighted that the King of Prussia had seen fit to entrust a valuable assignment into his hands.

It was dark when Jan retraced his footsteps up the path and struck a course south until he picked up the road from Marazion and set off in the direction of Penzance. There were few people about as he walked briskly towards the multitude of twinkling lights that lit up the ancient port of Penzance. He spoke to no one, fearful that he may be forced to abort his mission before it had begun.

Following John's instructions, he made his way up Market Jew Street, past the Militia building and on towards the White Lion Inn. He did not rush, forcing himself to saunter slowly past the shop windows, peering in occasionally as if he were looking for a bargain amongst the bric-a-brac that was on show. In the gathering gloom, he stopped outside the Inn. Despite displaying an air of casualness he was nervous. Taking a deep breath he went inside.

The bar was the biggest he had ever seen. It stretched from wall to wall backed by a variety of different drinks that Jan had never set eyes on before. Opposite, several booths had been built to give a degree of privacy for those who wished it. Jan was thankful that his presence caused only a perfunctory glance from those already in the room. They seemed to be more intent on filling their mugs than worrying about the arrival of a stranger. Jan leant against the bar and ordered a jug of ale that he knew was made on the premises. The bar tender duly obliged. Gulping down half the contents in one draught, he began to relax. A quick glance around satisfied him that there was no one of any consequence in the bar. A group of fishermen drinking and playing dominoes in one corner, a merchant seaman at the other end of the bar who had not removed his gaze from his glass and a couple in one of the booths intent only with their own company. The atmosphere was relaxed and convivial. He sipped the remainder of his beer and began to wonder whether it was worth a risk and engage the bar tender in conversation. Just as he was about to speak the door opened and in walked five uniformed men from the Militia. Jan nearly choked when he recognised Sergeant Crowlas.

"A bottle of Alsace and five glasses if you please," boomed the Sergeant.

The bar tender jumped to attention and speedily acted on the request. The Sergeant was evidently a man to be respected.

Jan buried his face as far into his glass as it would go and tried to look inconspicuous. The five men remained at the bar steadily sipping their French wine, holding a deferential conversation with their broad shouldered Sergeant until his voice rose above the murmur of conversation and, so the whole Inn could hear, he boomed, "Drink up men it will be your last chance for a while. We've a task to bring that murdering King of Prussia to justice. He's gone too far this time."

There was a murmur of agreement from the uniformed men. No one else spoke.

Jan's heart was in his boots, there could be no doubting it now, the guard had died and John Carter would be held responsible. He half wished it had been John who had killed the guard at least he could make a run for it. Now he was honour bound to Lord Godolphin to betray his own brother.

The soldiers finished the bottle of wine and, after purchasing another, left the Inn. Jan supposed they would continue their drinking in the barracks down the street where Jan and his comrades had sneaked past the previous evening.

He was left to brood over Sergeant Crowlas's remark. He could see no way out of it for the Carters. Although he did not hold much love for Henry Carter, he did not want to see him swing. Their only hope was to make a run for it and get out of the county before they were caught. His thoughts were cut short by the bar-tender who, having finished washing the dirty wine glasses, had shuffled to his end of the bar.

"It's a sad business, that's for sure," the bar-tender remarked.

Jan was determined not to be caught off guard. "What business?" He replied.

"Why the murder last night, haven't you heard?"

"No. I've been away for a few days. Tell me what happened."

Glad of someone to talk to, the bar-tender launched into a garbled account of the events that occured the previous night. Despite one or two discrepancies the gist of the account tallied with Jan's own. He was mildly relieved to hear that his identity had not been discovered by the pack of Militiamen that had chased them from Penzance to Godolphin House. It was clear to everyone from where the other rider came.

"And what of the poor unfortunate soul who was guarding the warehouse?"

The bar-tender stroked his chin. "Well, he was taken to the Infirmary at St. Clare and according to Sergeant Crowlas, he must have died."

Jan finished his drink and left. The claustrophobic atmosphere of the Inn was clouding his judgement. Once outside the fresh night air helped to clear his brain and, after walking a few paces he felt better.

Without choosing a particular direction, he walked up the hill towards the north side of town. He was lost in thought and was surprised to find himself standing outside the Infirmary. Without stopping to think he went inside.

A candle burned slowly on the reception desk in the hallway. Behind it, slumped an attendant, fast asleep. Jan slid past him and made for the glimmer of light along the corridor. St Clare's Infirmary was not a large building, catering for minor injuries and afflictions, anything of a serious nature would be despatched to the larger hospital in Truro. The only time the tiny ward would be full was when a disaster occurred at sea. The drowned would be laid out in a neat line on the floor ready for their loved ones to pay their last respects. Jan had heard tales about St. Clares from the fishermen who had first-hand knowledge of the salt-ridden bodies as they awaited identification. He had little doubt that the deceased guard would be lying in the same macabre state.

Nothing stirred in the corridor apart from the scuffling of a mouse as it searched vainly for an escape from the tip-toeing feet of Jan Pendray. He was nervous now, the first flush of confidence giving way to a sense of deathly apprehension. He had seen many dead bodies in the past, his upbringing having been littered with many painful happenings at sea. It was a way of life in Cornwall, but he was about to face a corpse that had been killed in cold blood. It filled him with nausea.

He approached the ward door with a modicum of respect, anxious that he should not disturb the poor man's eternal sleep. He peered through the glass panel in the door his eyes adjusting to the light. There, laid out on the cold marble slab was the body of a man. Already the signs of rigor mortis were apparent, his arms and legs rigid like the mast of a schooner, his cheeks hollow and sunken. Jan stared hard at the man transfixed by the deathly mask that hung over his face. His eyes were open staring aimlessly at the ceiling. It was not a pretty sight. Jan shuddered and fought back an awful feeling of sickness that was welling in his throat. He forced himself to look again at the shadowy figure on the slab.

There was no doubt in his mind, this was not the man he had seen emerge from the Guardhouse. The skin was wrinkled and salt clung to his matted hair. This was a sea-farer and the body had spent a long time in the water. Jan re-traced his footsteps, past the sleeping orderly and out into the street. He gulped thankfully at the cool night air. The Hospital had made him nauseous. It was different at sea, he could adjust to death with a more philosophical attitude but in the confines of a small, ill smelling room, the reek of death penetrated his soul.

"This gets stranger every minute," he mused.

Why was the body of the Guard not at the Infirmary? Could it be that Sergeant Crowlas was not as honest and straightforward as he led everyone to believe? Perhaps he was spreading false rumours deliberately to incriminate John Carter or perhaps he had moved the body to a more secure place. Whatever the reason, Jan was not satisfied, he had come to Penzance with the intention of getting answers and so far, he had precious little for his pains. He knew there was only one course of action to take.

The Militia house was a large granite building holding an imposing presence over Market Jew Street. It had no windows at the front and the only access was by a door that backed onto the street. Jan walked up to the door and gave the brass door knocker a resounding bang. Nothing stirred so he knocked again. At length a glimmer of light showed under the door. Jan heard the sound of the chain being drawn back on the inside. The door opened to reveal a man stripped to the waist and holding an oil lamp in his left hand.

"What do you want at this hour?" He demanded, a slight slur in his speech indicating that he was drunk.

"I'm sorry to trouble you at this time of night,sir, but I have lost my companion."

"Begad man! We're not a nursery. This is the Militia house not a home for waifs and strays."

He was not in a good humour, this was serious drinking time.

"But she is a young girl and I fear for her safety in a place like Penzance."

The Militiaman sniffed and his tone softened a fraction. "A girl you say, you had better come in and tell the Sergeant."

Jan stepped inside and followed the lantern down a corridor, up some stone steps and into a well-lit room at the back of the building. Seated around a large wooden table were seven men. They were all the worse for drink. At the head of the table sat Sergeant Crowlas.

"What have we hear, Vercoe?" The Sergeant asked addressing the man with the lantern.

"This man says he's lost a lady friend in Penzance tonight. He wondered if we had heard anything."

There were loud guffaws around the table.

"Probably down Ma Penberthy's place," one said causing more drunken laughter.

"More like on board the Skylark entertaining the ship's company." The Militiamen were enjoying themselves hugely.

"Wait a moment. Don't I know you from somewhere?" It was Sergeant Crowlas who spoke, his voice cutting into Jan like a knife. He felt the hairs on the back of his neck stand up and the beads of sweat break out on his forehead but he maintained his composure.

"Yes, you may well remember me for I saw you in the White Lion an hour ago."

Jan's heart raced as the Sergeant surveyed him keenly.

"Aye, yes, that must have been it. I knew I had seen you somewhere- I never forget a face."

Apparently satisfied he returned to his glass.

"I would be grateful if you could let me have any information about my sister if you hear anything. I know she has many wanton habits but I cannot stop worrying about her."

Jan turned to go, anxious not to give the Sergeant too long to study his face.

But the Sergeant had other ideas. "Sit down man, have a glass of wine with us before you go."

Jan had no alternative but to accept.

"Where do you come from, lad?"

""Falmouth, Sir, my father ran a small fishing boat out of Helford Passage. Since he died I have taken it over. It's a hard life but I enjoy it. I earn enough to feed and clothe myself and my sister. Anything left over allows us the odd trip to Penzance."

Jan stopped long enough to take a swig from the glass of wine that had been placed in front of him. It gave him courage.

"I hear that you are after the King of Prussia?" Jan asked the question with an exaggerated air of detachment.

The Sergeant stared at him keenly. "Aye, that we are, the murdering scoundrel accounted for the life of a warehouse guard- this time he has gone too far."

He crashed his fist down on the table with such force that the drink-crazed soldiers jumped to attention. In any other circumstance Jan would have found it funny.

"Do you know him?"

Jan replied quickly. "Yes or rather I know of him, his exploits are well known along the coast. My father said it was not wise to pry into his affairs. Too many people owe their livelihood to his patronage. I've heard he doesn't take to people meddling in his business."

"Well, this time he has gone too far. He has destroyed what respect he had by attempting a foolhardy escapade just to satisfy his own pride."

"So he knows the reason for the attack," thought Jan to himself his mind slowly grasping the implication.

"What of the man who was murdered?" Jan asked aloud. "I heard he was hit on the head."

"Dead, that's it," replied the Sergeant and said no more.

Jan let it drop he had already asked too many questions so he turned the conversation back to his mythical sister whom he so much wanted to find.

By this time the Militiamen were incapable, only Sergeant Crowlas appeared to be in control of his senses. Jan felt uneasy sitting next to him. He was a peculiar man, one moment he would give the impression of a well-meaning, conscientious keeper of the peace, the next he would take on the appearance of a man ill at ease with all around him. This lack of confidence led to violent displays of temper. Jan saw that he was lapsing into one of these morose moods and set about leaving the room.

Sergeant Crowlas had other ideas. "Let me tell you something," he slurred, pulling Jan back to his seat, "Never become a Sergeant in the Militia. There are things that work against you all the time. Justice is a myth."

He spat the last words out with such vehemence that Jan thought it wise to remain where he was.

"You work your way up through the ranks, sweat and toil for justice and fair play and what do you get? Nothing at all."

He turned his bloodshot eyes towards Jan. "I tell you, boy, there are forces working in this county that obstruct the cause of justice and what can I do about it? Tell me."

Jan wasn't sure whether this was a statement of condemnation of the King of Prussia or something of wider significance. In any event the question did not require an answer as the Sergeant had slumped forward and joined his men fast asleep over the table.

Jan finished his glass of wine and crept out of the room careful not to disturb the band of sleeping men. Once in the corridor he waited to let his eyes adjust to the darkness. He could dimly make out the bannisters of a narrow staircase that led to the floor above. Without thinking he crept stealthily up the creaking stairs. Each floorboard seemed to crack like a pistol under his weight. Nothing stirred in the darkness. At the top of the stairs he could make out four doors that led off the landing. Three doors led to unoccupied bedrooms and a small bathroom. The fourth was locked. Jan listened outside the door but could hear nothing. He paused for a moment and then entered the adjoining room. He slid silently across the room to the window and opened it. The sash cord held it high enough for Jan to lean out and touch the granite buttress that ran the length of the building. Without hesitating he hoisted himself through the window and onto the narrow strip of granite that separated him from the cobbled yard thirty feet below. With his back to the wall he inched himself along until he reached the window of the locked room.

Standing precariously on the window sill he tried to lever up the window. At first nothing happened, it refused to budge. He tried again and managed to move it enough to get his fingers under the frame and lever it open. Within a second he was inside. He stood there holding his breath. He was unable to see anything but he knew he was not alone. From somewhere in the room there was the sound of breathing.

Jan made his way carefully towards the rhythmic sounds. He was able to pick out the main features of a sparsely furnished room. A small bed was in the corner. On it slept a man with a white bandage on his head. Jan could scarcely contain his delight he felt this room held the key to the whole mystery. He was sure that this was the Guard who had supposedly been murdered by Henry Carter.

At that moment Jan was aware of the tramp of footsteps up the stairs. The drunken Militiamen were bedding down for the night. To Jan's horror he realised they would cut off his only means of escape. Frantically he scrambled out of the window and stood on the narrow buttress once again. Alas, he was too late, one of the drunken men had staggered to the open window and slammed it shut drawing across the latch. Jan was seized with an uncontrollable wave of panic. His legs turned to jelly and he started to tremble. His fingers clawed desperately at the granite aware that one false move would send him crashing to his death. With a mighty effort he forced himself to inch back to the open window. Clinging to the frame he was able to force his body back into the room with the sleeping man. He did not stir, blissfully unaware that his privacy had been invaded. Jan made another cursory glance at the turbaned guard and remained convinced that this was the man whom Henry Carter had attacked.

On the other side of the locked door a considerable amount of activity was taking place as the Militiamen conducted their drunken ablutions in preparation for an undisturbed night's sleep. Jan waited until all was quiet and then set about examining the lock. His scrutiny was cut short by another sound coming up the stairs. Jan shrunk back into the shadows as the heavy footsteps came closer. They stopped outside the door and Jan heard the unmistakable sound of a key turning in the lock. Jan hardly dared breathe. The door opened slowly and a shimmer of light penetrated the darkness. Sergeant Crowlas leant over the sleeping man, the lantern in his hand casting eerie shadows across the ceiling. He seemed satisfied and turned towards the door. As he did so the lantern swung round and a shaft of light caught the buckle on Jan's shoe. The Sergeant wheeled round in surprise.

Jan moved quickly, he smashed the lantern from his hand and sunk his fist into the Sergeant's belly. He groaned with pain as the blow sank into his bloated stomach but Jan's advantage was only temporary. Sergeant Crowlas quickly regained his composure and with a yell of anger, charged after the fleeing figure as it stumbled down the stairs. The other men, aroused by their Sergeant, appeared at the bedroom doors befuddled and confused. Cursing his men profusely Sergeant Crowlas led them down the stairs in hot pursuit. Jan, as if pursued by the Devil, arrived at the main door. Fortunately it had not been barred but not locked. Deftly he lifted the bar, opened the door and raced into the street. Throwing his head back he sprinted down the road towards the Causeway Inn. The air rushed past him ruffling his hair and filling his lungs. Behind he could hear the puffing and panting of the Militia as they charged after him. After his initial burst of speed Jan settled into a steady trot, confident that his stamina would be enough to see off his pursuers. However, he had not counted on the timely arrival of some horses. A group of merchants on their way home to St.Ives were forced to surrender their steeds to the imposing figure of Sergeant Crowlas.

At the sound of horses Jan veered off to the right and headed for the harbour. He forced himself into another punishing sprint. His feet pounded like pistons on the cobbles as they retraced the route of the previous night. Jan was desperately tired now and he could see his means of escape narrowing with every second. He pressed on until he found himself under the shadow of the Isles of Scilly lugger moored on Custom House Quay. He was trapped. The only means of escape had been cut off by the fast approaching horsemen. The leading rider gave a yell of triumph as he spotted Jan in the lee of the boat. Jan, realising that escape was impossible, slowly emerged from the shadows. The Militia, seeing this gesture of defeat, dismounted and walked cautiously towards him.

Jan had recovered a little of his breath but he wondered whether he could stand up to the ordeal his brain had suddenly presented as an alternative to surrender. With a yell of defiance, he turned and ran straight off the end of the quay, to the utter amazement of the Militiamen. He hit the water with a fearful splash, the cold water taking his breath away. Struggling with his shoes and jacket, he cast them off and set a course for St. Michael's Mount.

Few men have dared to attempt the swim across Mount's Bay, not because of the mere 4 miles distance but because of the wicked tides and eddies that are a scourge of the Bay. With three mighty oceans meeting in a crescendo of tortuous water it provided some of the most hazardous conditions in the world. Jan swam easily for the first hundred yards, the water acting as a tonic on his tired limbs. He knew no one would follow. The only risk he faced was the Revenue cutter. He hoped that the search would concentrate around the immediate foreshore between Penzance and Marazion.

Half way across Mount's Bay there is a small group of rocks that are barely visible at high water. Legend has it that a notorious giant was so overcome by the refusal of the lady of the Mount to take his hand in marriage that he hurled massive boulders into the sea in a violent display of temper. Jan thanked God for the strength of the giant as he made for the dark outcrops that offered the only sanctuary between Penzance and the Mount. Fortunately there was not a strong sea running and he was able to drag himself onto the seaweed clad boulders. He let the sea lap over his exhausted body. He heard the Revenue cutter put out to sea and saw a beam of light sweep across the dark water, he thanked God once more, the search appeared to be centred close to the beach.

He allowed himself the minimum of rest, afraid that any delay would result in his muscles seizing in the cold water. He fell into a rhythmic stroke his progress not helped by the constant presence of jellyfish that took great delight in feeding off the exposed parts of his skin. The stinging sensation was beginning to paralyse his legs as he continued his slow progress towards the Mount. When he could pick out the outline of the Mount towering up against the night sky, he headed left towards the shore. He was hardly swimming now, his energy completely spent as he drifted towards oblivion. He didn't care now and began to understand the stories of sea-faring men who said that drowning was the most peaceful way to die.

His path to eternity was interrupted by something solid. At first, his mind couldn't take it in. He had washed up on the Causeway that led to the Mount. He could hardly believe his luck, had the tide been in he would have washed right over the track and succumbed to a watery grave. He lay there utterly spent, if the Militia had arrived at that moment he would not have had the strength to walk let alone run.

All about him was peace, the only sound coming from the water as it lapped gently onto the sandy beach at the end of the Causeway. He was unable to move, happy to slip into oblivion his last thoughts fashioned by the eerie shadows of the castle. But he knew he must get up, the tide was coming in and soon his lifeline would be covered once again. Staggering to his feet he turned his back on the Mount and made towards the village of Marazion. He cut an unlikely figure tottering through the deserted village soaked to the skin and no shoes. Dawn was breaking as he made his way through Trescowe and down the path to the fisherman's hut he had left ten hours before. He did not dwell on the remarkable feat he had undertaken to escape the clutches of the Militia, content only to think about a warm place to sleep.

When he reached the hut he did not wait but staggered inside. It was deserted, Jan looked around in despair but his friend was nowhere to be seen. Perhaps he had been captured or worse still, gone to betray his brother. He fell on the pile of sacking in the corner his mind addled by exhaustion. He was asleep in an instant.

It was dark when he awoke, the last remnants of the day disappearing over the trees that lined the banks of the River Hayle. He was aware of someone else in the room.

"Well. Jan, I was beginning to think that you were never going to wake up," John Carter said in an amused drawl.

Jan blinked his eyes and picked out the familiar features of the man lying next to him.

"I've had a busy night," he replied wearily.

John had managed to obtain a liberal supply of food and drink from somewhere which Jan attacked ravenously. He was prepared to wait to see what news his compatriot had managed to procure. After watching him devour the last portion of fish pie, John could contain himself no longer.

"Well?" He said. "What news?"

Jan wiped his face with the back of his sleeve and launched into a detailed account of what had happened the previous evening.

John Carter said nothing, his only show of emotion coming when Jan recounted his swim.

"You swam across Mount's Bay?" He exclaimed in disbelief. "That was an almighty risk."

"It was either that or getting caught by the Militia. I preferred the sea."

John Carter was speechless. He shook his head from side to side before speaking softly, "Well, Jan once again I am in your debt. I never meant you to risk so much."

John was genuinely moved by the sheer courage of this mere boy who had exploded into his life with such force.

"What are we going to do now?" Jan asked, anxious to relieve himself of the burden of responsibility that had been thrust upon his young shoulders.

John Carter thought for a moment. "It seems that Sergeant Crowlas and the Militia of Penzance are not all they seem. But I cannot believe that they would have

44

set this all up on their own. There has to be someone else who wants to see the end of the King of Prussia."

"Who would want to risk such high stakes just to bring about your downfall?"

"Oh! There are plenty of people in the County who would like to see me out of the way. Some are jealous, others are worried that my trade is affecting their already overloaded purses. I can think of a number who fit the cap but I cannot imagine who would go to such lengths as "murder" and diabolical conspiracy.

CHAPTER 6

Exactly twenty-four hours after Jan's visit to Penzance, a large white horse trotted up the shingle drive that led to Pendennis House, its rider decked out in the finest military uniform. The rider was nervous. He did not like having to face Peter Pendennis, a man who was evasive, quick-tempered and the possessor of a tongue that left no one in doubt as to the superiority of his station. His father, Lord Pendennis was much more agreeable man.

He dismounted, tied his horse to the iron rail and rang the doorbell. He stood there nervously until a butler in a stiff white shirt answered and beckoned him in. The main hall was vast, the walls containing endless rows of oil portraits that recorded the family's history way back to Elizabethan times. He felt intimidated by the surroundings, Lord Godolphin's house was big but this was vastly superior. The butler led him to a set of double-doors that he opened simultaneously. The room was carpeted, with heavy chinz curtains draped to the floor and a shining mahogany desk positioned in such a way as to gain the maximum amount of natural light. Gazing out of the latticed window was Peter Pendennis. He did not turn around content, instead, to gaze out across Carrick Roads to St. Anthony Head on the opposite bank of the River Fal.

The butler coughed. "A Sergeant Crowlas to see you, Sir."

The door closed and Sergeant Crowlas stood rigidly to attention waiting for a response.

Pendennis kept looking out of the window. "I thought I told you not to come here," he hissed.

"I had to, sir. Something has gone wrong." The Sergeant stood there awkwardly.

"Someone knows about the guard," he continued. "They know he is not dead."

Peter Pendennis remained motionless for a second and then whirled round to face the hapless Sergeant. His eyes were blazing with anger and, not for the first time, Sergeant Crowlas wished he had never become involved with such a dangerous man.

"You blithering fool," he shouted. "This was the best chance we had to rid the county of one of its most persistent outlaws."

The Sergeant remained silent, still standing stiffly to attention. He agreed that it was high time corruption in the county was tackled but he was not sure that this was the sole reason for Peter Pendennis wanting to eliminate the King of Prussia. In his eyes lawlessness had a habit of starting from above. However, he knew he was in no position to argue, he had placed his future in the hands of the man in front of him and there was no escape.

Pendennis ranted for a full minute, cursing and swearing at the Sergeant for his stupidity. It wasn't until his energy expired that he began to calm down and become more rational. His voiced returned to normal. "Who was the person that discovered the Guard?"

"I don't know his name but I would recognise his face again, of that I am sure."

The Sergeant was eager to please. "I got a good look at him."

He did not add that the person concerned had actually been drinking his wine and escaped by swimming out of Penzance Harbour. He was confident that the boy had drowned but he dare not lie to Peter Pendennis.

"Well, Sergeant, you will find this man and make sure he does not talk because I intend to inform the Director of Prosecutions that John Carter should be held for murder. The Court will be held at Bodmin in one month's time under Judge Jenkin."

Sergeant Crowlas shifted uncomfortably. Judge Jenkin was a hard man. His notoriety had spread like wildfire after the trial in Taunton. A number of men were found guilty of smuggling, not a single plea for clemency was upheld. They were all hanged. The Judge had shown no mercy and his summing up left no doubt that he regarded smuggling as a crime against the King.

"But, surely, no court would hear a murder charge without a victim?"

"That, my dear Sergeant, is where you come in." Peter Pendennis smiled thinly. "You will attend the hearing and testify that the guard in question was sorely wounded and died on the way to the Infirmary. You personally saw him die and supervised the removal of the body to the graveyard at St. Clare where you helped to dig the grave. I shall see that a suitable headstone is made for the poor unfortunate soul- you will place it at the head of a grave. There should be no difficulty in finding a suitable place as the graveyard is full of unnamed resting places."

The Sergeant's jaw dropped.

"I can't do that," he stammered, "it's against the law. It's all very well bringing a smuggler to justice but to interfere with the true course of law- it's not right. I won't do it."

The face of Sergeant Crowlas hardened into a mask of determination giving an inkling of the true character that had elevated him to the position of responsibility he now held.

"I think you will, Crowlas. You have gone too far already." Pendennis spoke contemptuously aware of the hold he had over the luckless individual that stood in front of him.

"You are asking me to perjure myself in court, to state what is not true. My conscience will not allow it."

"My dear man, your conscience is your own affair, not mine. I cannot help it if you chose to follow a path of illegality just to further your own pitiful career."

Pendennis was beginning to enjoy the Sergeant's discomfort. He hated this type of person, someone who had adopted lordly airs well above his station and, as a result, thought he had a right to question the standards of such people as himself. The arrogance he saw in this type of person clouded his own attitude to life, blissfully unaware of the hypocrisy of his thoughts.

Sergeant Crowlas stood miserably to attention as he visualised his promising career crashing in ruins about him. Whoever Peter Pendennis may be, he felt he couldn't do it. And, yet, what was the alternative? If he refused Pendennis was sure to reveal all the dubious transactions that had taken place since he became embroiled with the wretched man. Trying to convince himself, he knew that perjury was only necessary because the King of Prussia was a bad man but that did not make it right. It was a simple choice: conscience or save his own skin.

"I suppose I have no choice," he sighed heavily. "But at the end of it I want no more to do with your evil ways. This is positively the last time."

Pendennis smiled and his tone softened to oily condescension. "I knew you would see reason."

Sergeant Crowlas turned to go.

"Wait!" Pendennis rasped. "That man who saw the guard must be found. See to it immediately."

Crowlas nodded without speaking, keen to get away from the man who held the Sword of Damocles above his head.

His horse was waiting on the drive and he rode off as fast as he could, anxious to distance himself from the alien world he had entered.

Pendennis stood at the window and watched him go, a faint smile playing on his lips. Things were going well despite one or two matters that needed attention. He was annoyed at the discovery of the guard, it meant, instead of quietly taking the man out to sea and dropping him overboard, he had to be kept alive until the spy was caught. He could not afford to take the risk of killing him yet. He was confident that the Sergeant would do his duty and find the man in question. It wasn't too difficult to trace a stranger in these parts.

CHAPTER 7

The hut was casting long shadows over the still water of the River Hayle as John Carter led Jan up the path towards Trescowe. They had talked at length about the best course of action but were unable to come to any definite conclusions. The only thing of which they were certain was that the King of Prussia was in danger of being arrested for a crime he did not commit. They both had hunches that it would be an act of a desperate man if the charges were pursued under the present conditions.

The important thing was to conceal Jan's identity from those who could recognise him. It did not take much working out that whoever was behind this intrigue would dearly love to know of Jan's whereabouts. Where Jan was to hide posed a problem for John Carter, he could not stay at Prussia Cove and many of his secret hideaways were too dangerous to contemplate. The only sensible option was for him to return to Falmouth. John Carter would pay a short visit to the Cove and meet him there later.

The two men walked carefully down the lane towards Bessies aware that the stakes had risen considerably. If either of them were caught it would be the gallows. They stopped outside the Kiddlewink, all seemed quiet. They went in.

Bessie was at the fireplace stoking up the Cornish range.

"Well damn me, if it isn't the Cap'n!" She boomed, shuffling towards them. "We thought you'm dead."

She was evidently delighted to see them.

"It'll take more than a few Militiamen to see the end of John Carter," he laughed. "We need food and a horse for Jan, here."

"Leave it to me, Cap'n. I'll see to it right away."

She left the room in a fluster, muttering words of relief.

The two men sat by the range and let the warmth filter through their damp clothes. They knew that with Bessie around they were safe for the time being.

She returned a few minutes later with two cups of steaming tea. John wrapped his hands around the cup and said, "when you get a spare moment, Bessie, can you send two Guineas and a bottle of Rum over to Ma Shaw in Trescowe and a case of wine to George Treharne, the butler at Godolphin House. They have served the King of Prussia well."

"Aye, Aye, Cap'n. I'll take it from the store you recovered from the Warehouse." Bessie winked. "You'll be glad to know the shipment was despatched to their normal destinations. Not one man was caught- all got home safely."

"I'm glad to hear that Bessie but I am afraid we have forces working against us that may take a while to sort out. We have not heard the last of this."

John yawned and turned to the tray of sweetmeats that Bessie had placed on the table. There was some home baked bread as well, which went down very nicely with the fine bottle of claret and after they had eaten their fill, they sat back in the easy chairs and relaxed for the first time since the raid.

Their moment of contentment was rudely shattered by the sound of hooves outside. Jan started violently but John put a hand on his shoulder. "Easy, Jan, we are safe here, Bessie will see to that. The horses are for you."

The door opened and in walked Henry Carter.

"The Lord has seen fit to bestow protection on you, brother- welcome home."

John smiled. "Maybe, but I like to think it was something to do with my own ingenuity as well as divine guidance. It's good to be back and see you again."

The two men clasped one another in a giant hug. Jan was dumbfounded. He had expected John to chastise his brother over the guard. Instead he greeted him with all the warmth he could show.

John gave a brief account of what had happened, ensuring that Jan's part was not overlooked. Henry listened in silence his face inscrutable apart from a look of surprise when he recounted the swim across Mount's Bay. When he had finished Henry Carter spoke.

"I knew I didn't hit him that hard, it was rumoured that he was unconscious and about to die. Impossible I only tapped him lightly, just enough to stun him."

Jan could see that Henry Carter was relieved, the rumours that he had died must have laid heavily on his conscience.

John Carter turned to Jan when he had finished and spoke with concern, "It is time you went, Jan. It is too dangerous for you to stay much longer. I'll wager that we will be having a visit from our Sergeant Crowlas before tomorrow is out."

Jan was reluctant to leave, a small part of his heart had already attached itself to Prussia Cove but he knew it was the only way. They had treated him as a true friend, he would not forget. Henry Carter spoke to him in a different tone now.

"Take the horse outside with the two saddle-bags strapped to the flank."

Jan shook hands with them both and, after providing a map of where he lived in Falmouth, turned on his heel and left. With a perfunctory glance at the horse he saddled up and cantered away from the Cove. Roughly, he brushed aside a tear. He was leaving a group of friends who had treated him with a kindness that he had not experienced since his father had died. However, he knew the dangers involved if he stayed. All that stood between the gallows and John Carter was the possibility that he could refute the charge of premeditated murder that hung around his friend's neck. It was vital that his identity was not revealed especially to Sergeant Crowlas.

On his journey back to Falmouth, Jan mulled over the events of the past two days. Somebody was playing a dangerous game. To frame a common smuggler was not too difficult but the King of Prussia? That was a different kettle of fish. Not only was he well known throughout the county but also, he was popular with both the gentry and the working classes. A case against him would have to be watertight. This concerned Jan, whoever was behind this, must be confident of a conviction, otherwise he would not risk so much. It was all very mysterious.

"And what about the upstanding Sergeant Crowlas, Pillar of the Establishment?" Jan thought to himself. Here was a man with an impeccable record of honesty, a servant of the Crown who was well known for seeing every accused person had a fair trial. If he could not be trusted, who could?

Jan's confusion remained all the way to Falmouth. However, with the dawning of a new day his spirits rose. Falmouth was alive with people as he dismounted in front of the Seven Stars Inn and walked slowly up the cobbled street towards his home. The narrow streets of the town gave him a feeling of security he never experienced elsewhere. This was where he played hide-and-seek amongst the tight lanes and alleyways. The shops spilt their wares onto the streets making it impossible to walk with ease. He savoured the familiar smells from the Bakery, Fishmongers and Tanners, to him this was home.

Leaving his horse tied to the rail outside the blacksmith's forge, he took off the saddle-bags and walked down a narrow alley-way that led to the waterfront. This too, was a hive of activity. The arrival of the Falmouth Packet from America had drawn a huge crowd. Jan meandered past the chains of men as they unloaded cases of tobacco and fruit from the country that had at long last, gained its independence from Imperial rule. He watched for a minute as the old ship was relieved of its cargo before turning towards some concrete steps that led to a doorway some twelve feet above the quayside.

Once inside his room, Jan dumped the saddle-bags on the floor and slumped into a large leather armchair which bore the signs of being considerably older than its occupant. Nonetheless it was comfortable and quickly lulled Jan into a long, deep sleep. A loud bang on the door woke Jan with a start. He blinked and sat up, the banging continued, this time much louder. Jan went to the door and threw back the lock. Outside stood a man of considerable presence, his tall, wiry body filling the entrance to the room.

"Your rent, Mr. Pendray," he stated, his tone almost apologetic.

"Ah, Mr Jose, come in won't you?"

"No, thank you, Mr. Pendray the rent for the last two months is all I require. I would be obliged if you can give it to me now then I can return to my wife and family."

"Ah, yes, well..." Jan hesitated. "I think I have some money here in my saddle-bag."

Jan made a gesture towards the bags that lay on the floor fully aware that he did not have the money to pay his landlord. He made a pretence of searching, while Mr. Jose stood patiently on the door step.

"I am afraid that if you cannot pay this time I shall have to inform the bailiffs and have you evicted. I don't like doing it but I have a family to feed and clothe. I am sure you understand."

Jan wasn't listening. Instead he had fixed his attention on the contents of the bags. To his utter amazement he found, wrapped in an old neckerchief, the princely sum of fifty guineas. He couldn't believe it. He had never seen so much money in his life. Looking through the saddle-bags had been a delaying tactic to give him time to invent an excuse. He never expected to find money inside.

Recovering quickly, Jan pressed five guineas into the hand of the surprised landlord.

"Will that cover it for a while?" Jan said with a grin.

"It certainly will, sir, thankyou very much. I'll not trouble you again for a while."

Touching his cap, he marched off down the steps humming to himself and jangling the guineas that were safely inside the pocket of his breeches.

Jan closed the door and returned to the contents of the saddle-bags. Apart from the money, there was a complete change of clothes, a bottle of Alsace wine, a pair of riding boots and a liberal supply of bread and cheese. Jan mentally thanked John Carter once again and tucked into the food, his spirits partially restored. The money meant that finding employment was not an immediate necessity. Instead he could afford relax and enjoy a full belly, something he had not been able to do since the death of his father.

For the first time in a while he thought of Anna. His heart fluttered, the old feeling was still there, it was impossible to erase her memory. Although he did not regret his alliance with the King of Prussia, his means had only temporarily met. He had no secure future and consequently, he could not expect Anna's father to entertain the notion of allowing him to pay court to his daughter.

After brooding for a while, he began to find the small room claustrophobic so, changing into his new clothing, he went out. The men had stopped unloading the Packet for the day and the quayside was deserted. Walking up the alleyway, Jan retraced the footsteps he had taken previously. He found that his horse had been fed and watered by the jovial Blacksmith. He pressed a guinea in the delighted man's hand and took the mount by the reins. The Blacksmith watched him go with a wry smile. He had known the Pendrays for years and in Jan he could see many traits of his father. That was why he allowed Jan to use the forge free of charge. He knew a Pendray would always honour his debts. Jan, in turn, was glad to be able to restore the family name. He was the only Pendray left now, it was important to him.

He guided the horse to the west of the town and onto the road that led to Constantine. As he approached the ancient cemetery he saddled up and took the bridle path down towards Swanpool. He was not sure how to engineer a meeting with Anna but he felt this overwhelming urge to see her. He craved for her touch, the very thought sending shivers of anticipation down his spine and his pulse racing. Blind love had taken away all logic from his life. He was going to see her come what may. He didn't care about her father's approval, she was the only girl he had ever loved and nothing was going to stop him.

Fortunately prudence did force him to admit that a direct approach to Merryn House would be foolish so he left the horse at the main gate and started to walk up the tree-lined avenue that led to the house.

He knew the area well. He had spent his youthful years around the beautiful house chasing rabbits, playing hide-and-seek amongst the lush green undergrowth. Before the house came into view, Jan veered off the drive and ploughed his way expertly through the bushes until he had circled the building and was able to approach from the rear. It was not yet dark but he could see a small candle glowing in the window of an upstairs room. Jan's heart jumped, it was Anna's room.

Careful not to disturb the servants' quarters on the ground floor, Jan picked up a handful of gravel and flung it at the lattice window. The clatter sounded like pistol fire. He froze astounded at the noise it made on the glass. Nothing stirred. He picked up another handful and was about to hurl it up when he saw a figure at the window. He caught his breath as he saw the familiar golden hair.

"Anna! It's me," he hissed.

She peered out of the window, unable to see the source of the voice.

"Anna, for God's sake! It's me, Jan!" He repeated.

She opened the window and peered out into the semi-darkness.

"Who's there?" She demanded.

Jan repeated for a third time. "It's me, Jan."

"Jan?" She gasped. "Is it really you? I thought you had gone for good."

"Not yet, can you come down?"

"No, it is impossible," she whispered her voice faltering. "My father would be very angry."

"To hell with your father, I must see you," he replied impatiently.

"I can't Jan, honestly, it's impossible."

"Just for a few minutes," he pleaded desperately. "I need to see you."

Anna hesitated for a few seconds and then said, "I'll meet you in the old summer house but only for a few seconds, my father will go mad if he finds out."

She disappeared from view. Jan made his way back to the line of trees and took the path to the summer house. Inside a minute he was sitting outside the old wooden building awaiting the arrival of Anna.

"Is that you, Jan?" A voice whispered out of the gloom. "Yes, over here."

She rushed forward and fell into his arms. He held her tight as the tears stung her eyes and her body wracked with uncontrollable sobs. He could feel the warmth of her body as she let the sorrow pour forth from her heart.

Eventually the sobs eased and they stood there motionless each taking comfort from the closeness they felt for one another. Neither wished the embrace to end lest the moment be lost forever. Entranced by the wonder of her touch, Jan kissed her gently on both cheeks.

"I love you, Anna," he whispered softly.

She turned away unable to look him in the eyes.

"I feel the same about you, Jan, but it will not work, it is impossible."

"It will work Anna, I promise. If you give me a little time I will prove to your father that I am as capable as any man of looking after his daughter."

. "Oh! Jan, dear, dear Jan!" She began to cry again. "You don't understand."

Jan was mystified. "You love me, don't you?"

She nodded vigorously but could not hide the sadness in her eyes.

"I do love you, Jan, but I am betrothed."

Jan started. " Betrothed? Who to?"

She hesitated and falteringly whispered the words that she knew would be like a dagger to his heart. "I am betrothed to Peter Pendennis."

His mouth fell open, completely unprepared for such a revelation.

"Betrothed!" He shouted.

"Don't get upset Jan, please," she pleaded. "It is for the best."

"Like hell it is," he raved. "Do you love him?"

"No, but...."

"Then why are you going to marry him of all people?"

He was really mad now, all the old prejudices over Peter Pendennis flowing to the surface once again.

"Be reasonable, Jan he is a man of good standing in the community and it will please my father to see such a match."

"Damn your father," he yelled. "Do you love Peter Pendennis?"

Jan grabbed her by the arms and shook her, his anger concentrated on a vitriolic flow of abuse aimed at Peter Pendennis.

Anna listened patiently to Jan's ranting. She knew that her words would cause Jan much pain. They had grown up together, she could read him like a book and the fact that it was Peter Pendennis, was always going to throw Jan into an uncontrollable fit of anger. She was desperately sorry for him but she knew that the barrier of wealth and class was insurmountable. Love was no match for the prejudices that ruled the conventions of life.

Jan could not understand this. He was naïve enough to believe that love could overcome everything. He was blind to the pressures Anna would be up against, the tattling women behind their fans, the disapproval of angry parents and, perhaps above all, the incessant fear of debt and poverty.

When Jan's anger had subsided, Anna spoke.

"Jan, I'm really sorry. Don't make it any worse. You will always hold a special place in my heart, you gave me more than any girl had the right to possess. I will never forget you, but I dare not go against the wishes of my father."

She was close to tears again.

"But, why Peter Pendennis? He's nothing but an arrogant fop. He will never make you happy."

"He is my father's choice. I know Peter is not perfect but he can see that I am well provided for and ensure that my life is conducted in the proper manner."

"Do you love him?" Jan spat the question once again with such intensity that Anna took a step back.

"What I feel does not count, he loves me. Any girl would jump at the chance of marrying such a distinguished member of society."

They stood facing each other hardly daring to breathe.

"Well, if that is what you want," Jan said heavily, "but mark my words, Pendennis will lead you a life of misery. Remember this day well, Anna, I will not pester you again. This will be your last chance to feel the love we had together".

He drew her close and kissed her gently on the lips. At first she drew back her trembling body betraying the turmoil she felt. But Jan would not let her go and, unable to stop herself, she responded to his kisses with a savage and forlorn passion as though this moment would never come again.

Much later, Jan picked his way through the trees and, finding his horse at the end of the drive, headed back to Falmouth.

CHAPTER 8

The following evening Jan got very drunk. It was not his nature to seek refuge behind a bottle but on this occasion, his spirits were so low that he needed something to take his mind off Anna. The Ship and Castle was a drinking place in the centre of Falmouth that found favour with all kinds of different types, from the hard drinking sailors to the genteel maid-servants who pursued furtive affairs with those of higher breeding. It was one of the few places in the town that cut across social barriers.

It was here that Jan found solace in a large bottle of Cognac. He sat at the bar staring into space and drinking himself into oblivion. The only person he spoke with was Meg, a nut brown beauty with a flashing smile and a generous nature. She ensured that his glass was never empty. She had seen it all from her position behind the bar but this one was different. She knew vaguely who he was. She had seen him on the quayside on a number of occasions. It worried her that she was unable to penetrate the mask. She prided herself on understanding her customers and giving them what they wanted. With Jan she could make no progress. After one or two abortive attempts to engage him in conversation, she withdrew to the other end of the bar where she knew her talents would be appreciated. Nonetheless, she was slightly irritated that such an attractive young man should show no interest in her.

Jan was relieved when she moved away, the task of holding a conversation was more than he could bear in his present mood. His besotted brain kept returning to the previous night's encounter with Anna and the revelation that she was going to marry Peter Pendennis. He had to admit that he never liked him but now that had turned to hatred. If he had stopped to analyse his feelings he would have realised that the prime reason for his hatred was jealousy. Pendennis had always had everything and now he was going to have the one thing Jan prized above all else. He felt sick, unable to come to terms with the injustice of it all.

He carried on drinking, dimly aware that the room had darkened as the last of the candles spluttered away in a mass of hot liquid. He was the only customer left in the Inn.

When he awoke the next morning, he was lying on a large, four-poster bed, his clothes neatly folded on the back of a wicker chair placed by the window. He blinked, unable to work out where he was or what had happened the previous night. The only legacy was a splitting headache and a mouth like a sailor's armpit. Jan levered himself up just as the door opened. It was Meg carrying a large tray.

"Breakfast for you, Mr. Pendray," she announced smiling down at him.

"You know my name?"

"Yes, there's not much I don't know about Falmouth."

Jan sat on the bed still unable to fathom how he had arrived in this situation.

"Did I get terribly drunk last night?"

"Aye,that you did. So drunk you fell off the stool and collapsed on the floor. It was all I could do to lift you up the stairs."

She smiled as she recalled the clumsy efforts he had made to walk.

Jan rubbed his eyes and yawned. "I am extremely grateful for your hospitality, I'm afraid you must have thought me ill company. I assure you I do not make a habit of it."

"You were certainly in no mood to talk last night. It was all I could do to get a grunt out of you."

Jan was embarrassed by the whole episode. He hated getting drunk and was always quick to condemn those who could not hold their liquor. It made his behaviour all the more abominable.

Meg sat on the side of the bed and watched Jan as he devoured the contents of the tray. She found him attractive in a peculiar way. He was too young to be considered good looking but the high cheekbones and the dark, swarthy skin common to the Celtic race, gave hint of the fact that he would soon mature into a highly desirable gentleman. What fascinated Meg the most was his unpredictability. After his morose behaviour of the previous night here he was all sweetness and light. She was pleased to see how genuinely grateful he was.

"I'm sorry but I don't even know your name?" Jan said, interrupting her thoughts.

"Meg, Meg Tremaine," she replied. "I own the Ship and Castle now, my husband passed away last year."

Jan was vaguely aware of who she was, it was something of a joke amongst the townsfolk. Meg had married old Josh Tremaine two years ago. They had been married for two months when he had a heart attack and died giving rise to a number of rude comments as to how he managed to last even two months with a woman forty years his junior.

Meg had ridden the criticism and sly remarks well and, although she inherited Josh's property, she did not have an easy passage. Running an Inn in such a busy seaport was difficult. Gradually she built up her own custom and began to gain the respect of the town becoming one of the most popular tenants on the waterfront.

Jan nodded his head when she divulged her name. "Ah, yes, I have heard about you but this is the first time I have had the pleasure of meeting you face to face."

Meg smiled. "Don't you believe all you hear about me, Jan Pendray. Things get exaggerated in a town like Falmouth."

Jan returned the smile. "I can assure you, all that I have heard is complimentary. My father told me lots stories about your late husband. He was a man of many parts and well loved by his friends."

"He was a good man," she replied affectionately. "I married him for love and nothing else despite what some people think. He was the most kind and generous man one could ever meet. I'll never find love like that again."

Jan noted she spoke with genuine affection. He was pleased. He was beginning to have a sneaking respect for a girl who could run a successful Inn in such a rowdy area. He finished his breakfast and pushed the tray aside.

"I must get up. I cannot impose on your hospitality any longer."

He swung his legs to the ground and sat next to her. She did not move, admiring his long, muscular legs that had appeared from under the bedclothes. She leant over and kissed him. Jan was not surprised. An unusual relationship had developed in an instant that did not require the usual social graces.

After leaving the Inn he sauntered down the alleyway to his lodgings. Despite a splitting headache and the traumas with Anna, he felt better for his night of drunkenness. The men on the quay were busily unloading the remainder of the cargo on board the Packet. He wandered between the crates and boxes that littered the wharf reflecting on the size of a vessel that plied across the hazardous waters to America. It was bigger than the Isles of Scilly boat but not much.

"About 300 tons," he thought as he surveyed the mast and mizzen of the clinker built vessel. "Just the kind of craft I would like to own."

He gazed in awe at the boat, captivated by the sheer magic and guts of a vessel that could ride the ocean with such alacrity. He debated whether the Captain would let him work his passage. He had heard tales of such wealth to be made in America since the granting of Independence.. It was, however, a passing thought and quickly dismissed it from his mind. If he had given it a second thought he might not have been so dismissive. Afterall he had nothing left in Cornwall.

His daydreams were interrupted by the cry of a newsboy who was selling copies of the Falmouth Advertiser. It was a broadsheet that grew up around the Packet, often carrying articles on the progress of the New World and giving details of those who had left the area in the quest for a new start. The cost of the newspaper was subsidised by the shipping company that used it as an advertising vehicle for the goods they transported across the Atlantic. It was not the adverts, but the cry of the paperboy that made Jan start.

"Read all about it, King of Prussia held on a charge of murder, read all about it!"

Jan rushed over and snatched a copy from his hand. Sure enough, in big headlines the front page read:

JOHN CARTER ALIAS 'THE KING OF PRUSSIA' HELD ON A CHARGE OF MURDER.

The article went on:

John Carter, the notorious smuggler from Prussia Cove was arrested outside the Customs Building in Falmouth and is being held at His Majesty's pleasure on a charge of murder. It was alleged that on the night of September 14th, he did enter the town of Penzance with a gang of men and did break into a warehouse, killing a guard in the process. In an ensuing chase, Carter escaped from the clutches of the Militia. His subsequent capture in Falmouth is a mystery. He showed no resistance to the arresting officers, Messrs Blakely and Harvey of the County Constabulary and an eye witness says he was smiling and declaring himself innocent of the charge.

The article went on to describe the background of the King of Prussia and ended with a short history of the arresting officers. Jan stared incredulously, re-reading it several times until he knew it by heart. It was too incredible for words, John Carter arrested and in Falmouth of all places. He put the newspaper in his pocket and ran back to the Ship and Castle.

"Meg! Where are you?" He shouted entering the back door that led to the kitchen.

"I'm in the taphouse," came the muffled reply.

He rushed into the yard and saw her emerge, hands covered in stale beer.

"Where would they take someone who has been arrested by the Constabulary?"

Meg wiped her hands on her apron. "More than likely they would hold him in the old courthouse in Fairmantle Street. That's where they take any customers who have had a drop too much. Why?"

Jan thrust the paper in her hand.

"Thanks, Meg, I'll see you later," he replied breathlessly and ran out.

The old courtyard had been converted into a prison at the turn of the century when the volume of offences became too great for the existing premises. Nowadays it was regarded as little more than a temporary stopping place for drunks and those who were accused of minor offences, hardly a place to detain an alleged murderer. However, it was the only prison in town so there was a fair chance that John Carter would be held there.

He ran up the road past the Moor and on towards Penryn. Just before the old ferry station that connected Falmouth with the castle at St. Mawes he turned left into Fairmantle Street. Halfway up on the left hand side stood a granite building similar to the Militia building in Penzance. The door was open so Jan marched in with all the authority he could muster. A small, squat man with a pair of rimmed spectacles sat at a desk in the foyer.

"Is John Carter being held on these premises?" He asked.

The little man was so absorbed in the book he was reading that he failed to hear Jan's question.

"Can I have your attention, sir?" Jan enquired, unable to hide his impatience.

Slowly the man raised his head and peered at Jan over his spectacles. "Now, my man, what can I do for you?"

"I am enquiring about John Carter, the King of Prussia. Is he here?"

The man closed his book and shuffled a few papers on his desk.

"John Carter you say? The name seems familiar, can't recall whether he is with us at the moment. We get a lot of overnighters, drunks mostly. John Carter- now let me see."

He ran his stubby fingers down a list that was on the desk in front of him.

"John Carter," he repeated. "Ah, yes, came in last night, must've been brought by the Constabulary because Mr. Harvey has signed the admission register."

"I would very much like to see him, if that can be arranged?"

The clerk shook his head. "Can't be done, no visitors allowed."

"But he is my brother," Jan lied. "I have travelled from Madron to see him."

"I have my orders, no visitors," the clerk replied vehemently. "It's more than my job's worth to let you see him."

"Would this help?" Jan produced a silver crown from his pocket and waved it in front of the diminutive person behind the desk.

His manner softened. "Well 'er, I suppose it wouldn't hurt- only a minute mind." His eyes were fixed on the shiny coin in Jan's hand.

Jan pressed the money into his hand and allowed himself to be led along a corridor and down some stone steps which led to the cellar. The air was dank and stale, condensation ran off the walls and it was cold. The only light and ventilation came from a small grating that opened onto the pavement above. Jan shuddered. "What a horrible place," he thought to himself.

"Two minutes, that's all, he's in that one there."

The clerk obviously disliked the atmosphere as much as Jan. He beat a hasty retreat leaving him alone in the slimy corridor.

There was an iron grill fixed to the door, Jan leant against and whispered, "John, John Carter is that you?"

The body that lay prone on the bunk slid quickly to the door.

"Jan, I knew you would come."

"How on earth did they come to arrest you? In Falmouth, of all places."

"It's a long story, Jan and I'm not at the bottom of it yet."

A cough came from the top of the stairs, the clerk was anxious to be rid of the visitor.

Jan leaned forward until his face touched the grill. "We don't have much time, is there anything I can do?"

John Carter spoke earnestly, issuing instructions in a quick and precise manner. Jan listened intently making sure he missed nothing. Another cough came from the direction of the steps.

John Carter finished his instructions and bid his friend farewell. "Goodbye for now, Jan, and don't worry they'll not hang the King of Prussia."

Jan did not share his confidence. "I'll do what I can but it will not be easy. You can rely on my word that I will do all that is in my power to help or die in the process."

John Carter took his hand through the bars and wished him well and then listened as his hopes of freedom went quickly up the steps from the gloomy cellar.

Despite his reluctance to leave his friend in such a miserable hole, Jan was thankful to breathe the fresh sea air once more. He nodded to the clerk on the way out, glad to feel the watery sunlight on his back. In daylight the problem seemed as massive as it did in the semi-darkness of the prison. He had pleaded with John to let him round up the men and spring him from jail but he would have none of it. He did not even want Jan to testify at his trial.

He retraced his footsteps and was soon sitting in his old leather chair staring out of the window. He could not understand why John did not want any of his men involved. With no witnesses for the defence there was no hope of escaping a conviction especially as the presiding judge was Justice Jenkins. The prosecuting council would labour the point concerning the raid to such an extent that the absence of any body would become irrelevant.

And what of Henry Carter? Would he allow his brother to shoulder the responsibility for a crime he did not commit? Jan had no misgivings.Henry Carter should be the one facing trial.

He was unable to sit for long, pacing up and down, brooding over the whole situation. Eventually the claustrophobic atmosphere of his tiny room overwhelmed him and he found himself back at the Ship and Castle. Meg was cleaning the bar when he entered, immediately she noticed the troubled look that clouded his features.

"No problem's too big to hide a smile," she said brightly.

"I'm afraid this one is," he sighed. " I can see no way out."

She put down her duster, poured two glasses of mead and led Jan over to the large window seat that looked onto the street.

"Do you want to tell me?" She asked gently.

Jan looked her straight in the eyes and sighed. "Yes, I think I do. You are the only one I can trust."

And with quiet relief he launched into an account of all that had happened, right from his first encounter with the King of Prussia up to the report in the Advertiser.

Meg sat silently, listening intently. When he had finished he looked up from his mead and waited for her to speak.

"I have heard many tales about the King of Prussia, his notoriety is well known throughout the county. He is well respected by both gentry and working men alike. I think that is his biggest asset. Do not underestimate the power of public sympathy."

"But what can I do, Meg? He does not want me to testify and I am one of the few who know what happened."

"Of course he does not want you to testify," she retorted. "You are running a grave enough risk by staying in Cornwall. He does not want you convicted as well."

Jan sighed heavily. "Maybe you are right but I don't like it."

"You have to accept it Jan, the sooner you realise that the quicker you can get on and carry out his instructions."

He knew she was right but it was hard. He took her hand and squeezed it. "Meg, I really do appreciate your understanding – thanks."

She blushed.

"And as for Anna," she continued, "I can understand her feelings, Cornwall is not a happy county to live in if all you have is a meagre pittance to keep the wolf from the door."

Jan remained silent unable to contradict what she had just said. If the truth were known, he had given little thought to his true love. John Carter's arrest had pushed his personal feelings to one side.

He stayed with Meg for an hour, drawing comfort from her practical approach to life. It gave him a new sense of encouragement. Just as he was leaving, Meg asked coyly, "did you really swim across Mount's Bay?"

Jan grinned and left.

Meg watched him go unable to explain the butterflies that seemed to be fluttering in her stomach.

CHAPTER 9

The next day Jan went back to Prussia Cove. The journey was uneventful apart from a few bands of roving Militia that he chose to avoid. It was not difficult as their horses gave ample warning, he had time to leave the road and let them go by. It was a wise precaution. Unbeknown to him, Sergeant Crowlas was searching the length and breadth of the County. When he reached the Cove he did not go down to the inlet but tied his horse to a gorse bush and headed for Bessies.

"What news of John?" She asked anxiously.

"I've been to see him in Falmouth. They are holding him there at the moment. I doubt if it will be long before they take him to Bodmin for the Assize next month."

Bessie wept. "How could they do such a thing? He has never hurt anyone in his life."

It was obvious that her concern was only for John.

"Is Henry Carter about? I must see him." He said changing the subject.

Bessie recovered herself and abandoning her brush, she hurried off in search of John's brother. She returned within five minutes.

"He will be here in a moment. He says to stay here and not to go out on any account."

Bessie, wheezing from the effort, picked up her brush and bustled out.

Henry Carter arrived a few seconds later.

"You can't stay here," his tone was grave. "Sergeant Crowlas has unearthed every stone and bush form here to Land's End looking for you. Your description has been posted in every town in Cornwall. You are lucky to have got this far."

His voice was sombre but not unkind, Jan noted that there was an edge of concern in his voice that had not been there before.

"I'll be as quick as I can. You already know that John was arrested in Falmouth two days ago. He will stand trial at Bodmin charged with the murder of the guard. I spoke with him yesterday and he is adamant. No one should speak on his behalf- not even you."

Henry Carter remained silent his face showing no indication of how he felt.

"All he wants me to do," Jan continued, "is to go to Truro and obtain a suitable lawyer. He says that you will provide the necessary capital."

Henry Carter scratched his chin and thought for a moment. "The day after you left for Falmouth, Crowlas and fifty men descended on Prussia Cove. They stayed all day, turning the cove inside out. We have since found out they were looking for you. He wasn't interested in John who he left alone. John thought he was safe enough while you were free, thinking they would not proceed with the case whilst a principal witness was still at large. He was obviously wrong. He was on his way to Falmouth to warn you to stay clear of the county for a few days. They must have arrested him on the way."

It was a long speech from Henry Carter but Jan could hear the obvious concern in his tone. Despite himself he warmed to the man.

"It's a funny business all round," sighed Jan. "I can't understand it."

"Someone must want the King of Prussia out of the way for a good reason," muttered Henry in reply. "And that someone must be high up to persuade the Constabulary to arrest him on such flimsy evidence."

Henry Carter moved to the door. "I'll be back in fifteen minutes, in the meantime do not show your head outside this door. There are one hundred guineas waiting for any person who can shed light on your whereabouts, enough to turn most heads around these parts."

Jan sat down and waited. The knowledge that he was worth 100 guineas had jerked him out of his complacency. This wasn't a game any more. He smiled grimly to himself determined to do all he could to save his friend from the gallows.

Henry returned with a letter addressed to Pendarves Bank, Truro. It was sealed. He took the letter and placed it in his coat pocket.

"Pendarves Bank is in Lemon Street. They will provide you with the necessary funds."

He took Jan's hand and added, "May the Lord go with you, Jan Pendray, I've a feeling you may need it."

Jan's reply was brusque. "Thank you, I will do all that is in my power to see that your brother is acquitted."

He was annoyed at Henry Carter's lack of concern for his brother's safety but could not bring himself to confront him on the issue.

He stepped out into the pale sunlight and mounted his horse. Unknown to Jan, Henry had cleared the smuggler's route out of the Cove so, despite him thinking that Militia lurked behind every rock, the journey away from the glistening sea was without incident. The red glow of the sunset cast long shadows across the autumn hedgerows as he headed inland and, making a detour around Helston, it was long past nightfall when he reached Falmouth once again. He tied his horse in the usual place and climbed wearily up the steps to his room. Pinned to the door was a note. By the light of the moon he was able to distinguish the words:

Jan must see you urgently, Meg.

Short and concise, it left Jan in doubt as to the serious nature of the scrappy piece of paper. Without bothering to open the door to his room, he went straight to the Ship and Castle. Meg saw him enter and instantly ushered him into the small sitting-room at the back of the Inn which she reserved for herself and a few chosen guests.

"Have you seen this?" She asked, producing a sheet of printed paper from beneath a cushion.

A REWARD OF 100 GUINEAS FOR ANY PERSON WHO CAN SHED LIGHT ON THE WHEREABOUTS OF A MAN WHO BROKE INTO THE MILITIA BUILDING IN PENZANCE. BELIEVED TO BE AN ASSOCIATE OF JOHN CARTER HELD FOR MURDER.

The man concerned is approximately 5`11``, aged between 19 and 23, long, dark hair, clean shaven and is believed to have a sister residing in the Falmouth area. Any information about this person should be passed to Sergeant Crowlas of the Falmouht and Penzance Militia.

Jan read it through twice and grinned.

"Where did you get this?"

"It was pinned to the noticeboard outside the Council offices but I have seen others all over town. Meg was visibly upset.

"Take it easy, Meg," he said soothingly. "From that description no one will recognise me. The description could fit hundreds of men in Falmouth."

"I'm not so sure. 100 guineas is a lot of money and it's sure to start tongues wagging. I think it would be wise to lay low for a couple of days."

"I can't do that, Meg. I must go to Truro and hire a lawyer for John."

Meg sighed and gave him a worried look. "Well, so be it, but remember, I shall be here if you need me."

Jan smiled affectionately and gave her a hug. "Meg, you are a wonderful woman and I do appreciate your concern but you have done more than enough for me already."

Meg stared up at his face, concern etched in her own. "You may not believe this, Jan, you are the first person to show me genuine affection since my dear husband died. I shall always remember that."

It was unusual for Meg to divulge her feelings in such a way but this young man had swept into her life like a tornado and she did not know how to deal with it. Jan left quickly, sensing that his own mask might slip but it was too late as far as Meg was concerned she had seen the look in his eyes. He may not understand but she did.

The next day Jan awoke to a chorus of seagulls that were perched precariously on the window ledge outside. He didn't mind, it reminded him of his birth right and with the smell of the sea in his nostrils, he set off for Truro. There were plenty of travellers on the road, merchants, gentry and tradesmen, all anxious to enjoy the benefits of market day in the big town. Jan kept his collar up and let his neck sink into the depths of his greatcoat. He was confident no one would recognise him especially as he was travelling northwards away from Penzance, but he was not taking any chances.

It took him an hour of hard riding before he eased his horse down the steep hill that led to the centre of the town.

Pendarves Bank was situated a quarter of the way up Lemon Street, an unmistakable building with large white pillars covering the pavement. He tethered the horse to the railing outside and stared at the building. Its imposing façade with the whitewashed pillars and the granite facia, gave it a bleak, almost frightening appearance. Jan had never been inside a real bank before and he found it intimidating. Summoning up every ounce of courage, he took a deep breath and crossed the portals. There were several booths free. He chose the nearest and handed the letter to a bespectacled man who was counting a large pile of change that he had stacked in front of him. He gave Jan a long, cold stare. He was not pleased that his counting had been interrupted. Jan returned the glare with calculated indifference waiting for the clerk to act on the contents of the letter. He was not a man to be hurried, he went back to his counting and, after what seemed an interminable time, cast his attentions to the letter.

"John Carter, eh?" He said after reading the contents. "He'll need more than this to help him where he is going."

News had evidently travelled fast.

"If you will be kind enough to settle this matter I will be on my way," Jan replied refusing to get drawn on the subject.

He re-read the letter.

"I need some proof of identity."

Jan, anticipating the clerk's demand, produced a gold watch and chain from his pocket.

"I have this."

It was the one his father had given him just before he died, on it was inscribed the words: 'To Jan Pendray. Time heals.' A remark to remind him of his lack of patience and the death of his mother.

The clerk scrutinised it closely, his beady eyes quick to notice the value of the timepiece.

"Sign here," he barked looking Jan up and down. Jan signed the paper quickly, anxious to be away from such an imposing building.

The clerk unlocked a cabinet beneath his desk and counted out a bundle of notes and passed them over. Peering beneath his spectacles, the clerk watched Jan go and then hurriedly reached for the 'Booth Closed' sign which he placed on the desk.

Jan drank in the fresh air outside the Bank. He had never felt so uncomfortable before. He did not like the manner of the clerk. He put his nervousness down to the colossal nature of the task in front of him but couldn't help feeling uneasy. He walked briskly down to the centre of town and turned his attention to the next piece of business.

By now it was midday, the sun was shining and a multitude of enthusiastic people were converging on Market Square. The majority were farmers bringing their wares to sell, but there were also a number of merchants and dealers who had come to attend a sale of antiques from the Civil War, which had been offered for sale by the owner of Landolph House. Jan was pleased to see so many people, he felt less conspicuous, he even indulged in a cup of China tea at the Roundhouse before moving on to the offices of Bannock, Rowse and Hart.

The girl who received him provided more of a welcome than the Bank. She was glad to talk to someone who was not a portly farmer or a middle-aged businessman.

"I would like to see a solicitor," Jan said briskly. "The best you have."

"They are all the best," she replied with a demure smile.

"I'm sorry," he replied, realising he sounded rather brusque. "If it would not be too much trouble, I would like to see one of your employers as a matter of some urgency."

She looked at the young man in front of her and tried not to laugh. It wasn't often that one so young required the services of such a distinguished firm of Solicitors.

"I think Mr. Hart is free, I will go and check."

She glided away from the desk and up the stairs with a flowing grace that did not escape Jan's notice. She returned quickly.

"Mr. Hart will see you now."

Jan followed the girl up the stairs, fighting back a mischievous desire to imprint his hand on the shapely bottom before his eyes. She knocked discreetly on a door at the top of the stairs that bore the title Mr. T.H. Hart in bold, black letters.

"Come in," a voice sounded from within.

Jan was led into a tiny room with barely enough space to allow more than three or four people in at one time. Around every wall there were row upon row of leather bound books. The girl squeezed past Jan and left him alone in the room with a youngish gentleman not much older than himself.

"Good morning, Sir, please be seated." He beckoned Jan to a chair that was placed before a heavy walnut desk. "What can I do for you? Nasty landlord? Gambling debts? Irate husbands? Or in trouble with the Authorities?"

"No, it is more serious than that." Jan replied. "I take it I can talk to you in the strictest confidence."

Mr. Hart stared at him, the faint smile doing nothing to betray the innate intelligence and shrewdness with which he was blessed. Even though his burgeoning reputation had been made on frivolous cases, he had climbed the ladder of success with great rapidity.

"You may speak freely here, I give you my word."

Jan liked him without knowing why. His senses told him that this mere youth was not sufficiently experienced to take on a case as important as this. All the same, the man had something, his air of casualness and lazy smile did not conceal the stature and bearing of a person whose resolve and uncompromising attitude had won many cases when a lesser man would have given up. Jan had no choice but to risk it.

"I have a client who needs the services of the best lawyer money can buy."

Mr. Hart continued to smile but said nothing.

"I have the money here. You will be paid in full."

The lawyer lent forward and looked at the money Jan had placed on the table.

"To whom do I have the pleasure of addressing?" He asked quickly.

Jan stammered. "I'm sorry. My name is Jan Pendray and I come from Falmouth."

"And who is your client?"

Jan took a deep breath before whispering softly, "John Carter."

For the first time Jan noted a chink in the inscrutable mask.

"He has been accused of murder. A crime he did not commit."

"I am well aware of the case, Mr. Pendray, indeed all of Cornwall seems to be talking of nothing else."

"Then you will take the case?"

Mr.TH Hart pushed back his swivel chair until it touched the rows of books stacked behind him.

"I will need to know more details of the case. Does Mr. Carter realise that the presiding Judge is none other than Judge Jenkins?"

Jan nodded. "I have heard he does not like smuggling."

"He is the scourge of all illicit traders. He has sent more men to the gallows than any other presiding Judge in England."

Jan's face fell. "So you won't be taking the case?"

"I didn't say that," Mr. Hart replied quickly. "I will need to know everything that you know."

Jan spent the next twenty minutes relating what had happened to John Carter and the evidence that was stacked against him. He took care not to mention Henry Carter by name nor did he offer any reason as to why John Carter had been framed. He finished by saying, "you will understand that my position is delicate, it is possible that I could be arrested at any time so I beg you to take the case before it is too late."

He had never begged to anyone in his life but he was desperate, without a lawyer John Carter's fate would be sealed.

Mr. T.H.Hart sat there his face expressionless. Silence reigned in the room, Jan could hardly breathe. At length the lawyer spoke.

"Just supposing I believe your story, no one in their right mind would bring a case of murder against a suspect unless there were witnesses and the body had been properly identified."

"There are forces working in this county that have no respect for law and order, Mr. Hart, I cannot explain what is happening in this case but I do know that John Carter is innocent."

Mr. Hart gazed steadily at Jan, his fingers drumming quietly on the blotting pad in front of him.

"You realise, Mr. Pendray, that any lawyer taking on this case would have little chance of success. The Crown does not bring cases to court unless they are certain of securing a conviction."

"That is not a reason for not trying," Jan replied, throwing his hands up in frustration. "He is innocent, that should be enough."

Mr. Hart's mind was working overtime behind his calm exterior. He knew there was little chance of saving John Carter's neck even if Pendray was telling the truth, which he very much doubted. What did appeal was the status and publicity he would obtain from being associated with such an important trial.

Finally he said, "I will take the case."

Jan heaved a huge sigh of relief. " Thank you, sir," he leaned forward and grabbed the lawyer's hand. "You won't regret it."

Mr. Hart smiled in amusement at the intensity of the handshake.

"My secretary will settle the details and I shall visit Mr. Carter when he is transferred to Bodmin Jail.

"Thank you once again, sir," Jan repeated and got up to go.

"There is just one other thing, if what you say is true, there must be someone working against Carter, have you any idea who that might be?"

Jan hesitated before saying, " it is a question I have asked myself a dozen times, all I can say is that it must be someone in the highest circles if he is able to influence a Sergeant in the Militia."

CHAPTER 10

The day of the trial was provisionally fixed for October 14th assuming the pressure on the court was no greater than it normally was for that time of year. Jan had made his way to Bodmin on the previous day booking into the Angel Inn well before the allotted time for supper. He was travel-weary but in good health having spent the last few days with Meg doing little other than eat, sleep and keep out of the way of prying eyes.

Having unpacked his few belongings, he went downstairs to the bar. The Angel, being the only hostelry of note in the town of Bodmin, was patronised by working class and gentry alike. It seemed to Jan that the whole of Cornwall had come to attend the trial, the streets were packed with people and the overflow from the bar spilled onto the pavement. Everywhere the topic of conversation was John Carter, King of Prussia. Jan elbowed his way to the bar and ordered a beer. Secure with his drink, he manoeuvred himself to the comparative calm of the dining room. Glancing around, he chose a small table by the window affording a good view of the mass of humanity outside.

The waiter was admirably quick with his order so he was able to sit back and observe the jostling throng. His reflections were cut short by the mention of his name. He looked round quickly to see that the source was Mr. T H Hart.

"May I join you, Mr. Pendray?" He enquired politely.

Jan was delighted to see a friendly face. "Certainly, please sit down. I was hoping to catch you before the trial."

Mr. Hart pulled up a vacant chair and lit a small clay pipe that he produced from the top pocket of his waistcoat.

"I have had a talk with our client and it seems he is prepared to do very little to help himself. He refuses to allow anyone to testify on his behalf and was reluctant to accept my advice. However, we did come to an amicable, if not wholly satisfactory, understanding. He will allow me to advise him on the code and practice of law while he conducts his own defence."

Jan sighed in exasperation. "I suppose I should have expected that. He wants to make sure that all the guns are pointing at him. He would rather die a martyr than implicate those close to him."

"Martyr might be too strong a word, Mr. Pendray, although he carries a considerable body of opinion on his side, there are and equal number of influential people who regard smuggling and murder as abhorrent. I'm afraid that the charge of murder will have to be disproved if he is to have any chance of winning wider public sympathy. Remember Judge Jenkin is a hard and inflexible man and not likely to be influenced by the vocal minority that will pack the public gallery tomorrow."

Jan picked gloomily at the platter of food that had been placed in front of him exchanging pleasantries with the lawyer. When he had finished he wiped his mouth on the linen serviette and glanced out of the window. It was getting dark and the grey clouds that scudded across the gloomy sky gave warning of an impending storm. Suddenly he started with such violence that Mr. Hart nearly choked on his soup. Outside, amongst all the riffraff, Jan saw the distinct figure of Sergeant Crowlas. At his side was a person Jan knew well, Peter Pendennis. They were in deep conversation barely aware of the mayhem around them.

Realisation began to dawn on Jan. This was too much of a coincidence. Pendennis here and talking to Crowlas, it all began to make sense. He recovered quickly and apologised to the mystified lawyer.

"I am sorry, Mr. Hart, but there are two gentlemen out there who you will encounter in the future. The one in uniform is Sergeant Crowlas of the Penzance Militia who has put a price on my head, the other is none other than Peter Pendennis."

Mr. Hart leant forward and peered through the window. By their stature and the clothes they wore, it was easy to pick out to whom Jan was referring.

"Sergeant Crowlas I have not seen before but Pendennis I recognise. He often comes into Truro with his father, although rumour has it, he travels little further than the lounge of the Red Lion."

Jan sat on the edge of his chair staring out of the misty window. "I'm sure he is behind all this. It would take someone like him to turn the head of Sergeant Crowlas."

"Your client did say that someone had a grudge against him but he did not know who."

"It all makes sense now, the raid on Prussia Cove, the attempts to blacken the name of John Carter. Pendennis is up to something."

The two men outside had disappeared from view leaving Jan in a high state of animation. He ordered another beer. "Surely Pendennis wouldn't go this far. Accusing someone of murder is a grave matter."

Mr. Hart finished his meal and watched the reaction on Jan's face with detached amusement. "You don't like Pendennis do you?"

Jan stiffened. "I hated the bastard, all my life I have been in the shadow of that arrogant brat. We grew up together, We even went to the same elementary school. He never missed a chance to ram home the fact that he was from a higher station. But I did not think he would stoop to this."

"He is taking a grave risk if what you say is true, but the Pendennis name carries considerable weight in the County. Money and Class have a habit of securing most things these days."

Jan was gripping his glass with such force the whites of his knuckles were clearly visible.

"Mr. Pendray, may I offer you some advice?"

Jan wasn't listening.

"I suggest Mr. Pendray, that you leave Bodmin immediately. You are irrational as far as Pendennis is concerned and Sergeant Crowlas is after your blood. Your presence here will not aid Mr. Carter's cause and may hasten your own demise."

"No! That I will not do," he replied vehemently. "John Carter is a friend. I do not intend to desert him now."

Mr. Hart shrugged his shoulders and sipped his wine. He had seen the flames burning in his eyes and recognised that it was useless to argue. If he wanted to precipitate his own downfall then so be it, he had a case on which to concentrate.

Jan left the table and went back to the crowded bar. He bought a bottle of claret and elected to drink it in the privacy of his room. As he was waiting for his room key from the reception desk, he glanced idly down the list of guests staying in the hotel. He was not surprised to see the name of Henry Jenkins amongst them. He also noted the name of Sergeant Crowlas but not Peter Pendennis. He climbed the stairs warily, aware that his stay in the hotel had suddenly become uncomfortable with the presence of Sergeant Crowlas. However, he reached his room without interruption. Once inside, he locked the door and took a long swig from the bottle.

At three a.m. the candles in the corridor were burning low, casting eerie shadows across the yellowing walls. Jan left his room and tip-toed down the corridor, stopping at the top of the stairs. He listened intently. Nothing stirred in the hotel, only the spitting of the candle wax broke the silence. He crept up the stairs until he was on the floor directly above his room. Peering closely at the numbers on the doors, he glided swiftly along the corridor until he reached number 16. Here he stopped and placed his ear to the door. At first he heard nothing above the pounding of his heart, but gradually, he was able to pick out the sound of rhythmic breathing from within.

Using both hands, he gently turned the handle. Stifling a sigh of relief he found it was not locked. He opened the door a fraction. A solitary ray of light from the candle in the corridor danced across the room and silhouetted the profile of a large man as he lay snoring on top of a four poster bed. Moving quickly he produced some fishing line from around his waist and bound the man's wrists and ankles to the bedposts. The sleeping man did not stir. Inside a minute he had bound the arms and legs securely to the solid frame of the bed. He then lit a candle that was on the bedside table. The flame grew slowly casting flickering images across the bed. Moving on to the washing bowl he scooped up a mug full of water and threw it into the face of Sergeant Crowlas.

The Sergeant opened his eyes with a start.

"We meet again, Sergeant Crowlas," Jan said smoothly.

The poor Sergeant, still dazed with sleep began struggling with the bonds that held him to the bed. It was no use, Jan had secured them well.

"What's happening, who are you?" Sergeant Crowlas was beginning to realise the extent of his predicament.

"My name is Jan Pendray, I believe you are looking for me."

The Sergeant continued to struggle. "Untie these knots at once."

Jan, who had remained in the shadows at the foot of the bed, moved closer.

"Now do you recognise me Sergeant?"

Recognition gradually dawned on the Sergeant as he picked out the face that had been haunting him for the past three weeks.

"I arrest you, in the name of the law!" He tugged violently trying to force himself free but it was to no avail.

Jan laughed softly. "I don't think you are in any position to arrest me Sergeant."

"If you do not untie these immediately I will call for help."

"I don't think that would be wise, Sergeant, you would not want your position as chief witness for the Prosecution to be compromised in any way."

The face of Sergeant Crowlas contorted in anger as he renewed his efforts to free himself.

"You may have sided with John Carter," he snarled, "but it won't do you any good, he'll swing for certain."

"He won't if you tell the truth."

"Why should I save the King of Prussia, he's a no good outlaw and brigand who was bound to get caught in the end. What difference does it make?"

"It makes all the difference, Sergeant. There is a world of difference between a little illicit trading and murder." Jan was getting angry, he came closer.

"If you commit perjury in order to secure the downfall of John Carter, I will personally see that your body is cut up into a thousand pieces and fed to the fishes."

For the first time, Sergeant Crowlas noted the expression on Jan's face.

"Now let's be reasonable about this, untie me and we can talk about this sensibly."

"No deal, Sergeant, I prefer to have the odds stacked in my favour for a change. You have already forced me to swim across Mount's Bay and it seems that I cannot walk the streets without fear of arrest."

Jan was deriving a certain satisfaction from seeing the unfortunate Sergeant crawl.

Sensing a chink in Jan's armoury, Sergeant Crowlas said, "I give you my word, I will see that you are able to leave Bodmin a free man and the search will be called off."

"Still no deal, Sergeant, I doubt if you would bother to search for me after the trial anyway. You only want me because I am the one person who knows that you will be lying when you take the stand tomorrow. Don't you have any conscience, Sergeant?"

The Sergeant winced at this last remark. Jan had found his one weakness in the whole sordid affair. He had been fighting his conscience ever since his meeting with Peter Pendennis. He did not need a young upstart to labour the point.

Jan saw he had scored a hit. "Conscience is a funny thing, Sergeant," he continued,. "especially when it is brought about by greed. Is it worth sacrificing your career for a man like Peter Pendennis?"

This really did shock the Sergeant. He had no idea that anyone knew about his association with Pendennis.

"How do you know about him?" He stammered.

"Never you mind. Enough to say that I know he is behind all this and I want to know why."

The Sergeant went white. "I can't tell you anything."

Jan moved closer until his nose was almost touching the stubble on the man's chin. "I don't believe you," he said softly. "Perhaps you need a little persuading."

He drew a knife from his waistband and let the blade glint menacingly in the shallow light of the candle. Beads of sweat began to appear on the forehead of the Sergeant, seeing the look on Pendray's face, he had no doubts that he was capable of using such a menacing weapon.

Jan drew the edge of the knife gently across the neck of the perspiring Sergeant, making sure that he felt the full effect of the cold steel on his skin.

"Why, Sergeant Crowlas?"

The blood was beginning to trickle down the Sergeant's neck, congealing in an untidy mess on the collar of his nightshirt.

"I don't know, honestly, for pity's sake," Croaked the Sergeant as the combination of blood and sweat exaggerated the slight cut to such an extent that he thought he was bleeding to death.

Jan held the point of the blade so that it rested on the bridge of the Sergeant's nose. He rocked it back and forth allowing it to penetrate the delicate skin below the eyes. The poor individual's eyes were nearly falling out of their sockets in terror.

"For God's Sake! You'll kill me. I know nothing about Peter Pendennis."

Jan took the blade away for a moment. "He must have wanted the King of Prussia dead very badly to risk perjury. I hope you think sacrificing your precious conscience for a rat like Pendennis is worth it."

Sergeant Crowlas' resistance collapsed. "All I know is," he wailed, "he promised to put in a good word for me at the next meeting of the Constabulary board, in exchange, I would have to testify against John Carter. If I had known in the beginning how it was going to turn out I would not have gone through with it. I swear it."

Jan returned the blade to the broken man's face, a little rivulet of blood began to trickle down the cheek and enter the corner of his mouth.

"I'm inclined to believe you, Sergeant, but...." Jan pressed the blade deeper. "If you make that false statement..." His voice trailed off, leaving Sergeant Crowlas in no doubt as to the consequences of his actions.

CHAPTER 11

Jan awoke the next morning with a splitting headaches and a parched mouth. It was a salutary reminder of the rashness the wine had produced in the night. He doubted whether the threats would do any good, but he took comfort from the fact that he had, at least, made Sergeant Crowlas come to terms with his conscience. He had taken pity on him and slashed the binding on one of his wrists before he left, he was confident the Sergeant had too much to lose in pursuing the matter any further.

Breakfast was a sedate affair. Neither Mr. Hart nor Sergeant Crowlas appeared but Jan did notice the Honourable Henry Jenkins who was sipping coffee and reading a copy of yesterday's Times. Jan completed a leisurely breakfast and wandered onto the street. Even at this early hour Bodmin was alive with people. The previous day's cloud had given way to intermittent sunshine and, although there was a nip in the air, the atmosphere had brightened considerably. Jan strolled idly down the main street gazing into the tiny shops that catered for the needs of the moorland people wondering how such a tiny community could support such an array of produce.

The trial was due to start at 11 o'clock. Jan made his way towards the Assize Court in ample time to secure a seat in the public gallery. It was a wise move as the gallery was already half full, by the time 11 o'clock came, there was not a spare inch to be found anywhere in the courthouse.

A hush of expectancy came over the Court as the case against a poor unfortunate wretch who stole his neighbour's chickens was brought to an abrupt end with a one year prison sentence. Jan felt the tension arise around him. They had all come to see John Carter in the flesh. Rumours about the King of Prussia were rife throughout the county, now it was their chance to judge for themselves. A door opened to the side of the vacant Judge's chair and flanked by two wards of court, in walked John Carter. Excited whispers broke out all round the public gallery as they focused their attention on the notorious smuggler. Jan was surprised at how well he looked. He had shaved and wore a finely cut suit. He gave a dashing smile to the gallery.

A cry went up from the back of the room. "John Carter is innocent!"

"Long live the King of Prussia!" cried another.

Jan stared around him. Dotted about the throng were several faces he knew. It raised his spirits. At least John could see he was not alone. The sporadic support swelled into a crescendo of noise as others joined the mantra for the King of Prussia. Not a single voice was raised in support of the King's council. The harassed clerk of the court began to sweat profusely. He had never witnessed such scenes in a court of law before.

"I shall clear the court," he cried lamely but his words were drowned by the chants from the public gallery.

The door at the front of the court opened and in walked the solemn figure of Justice Henry Jenkins. Immediately the crowd went quiet. He stood silently by the bench staring at the rabble. There was an uncomfortable silence as he met each person present with an icy glare.

"Any more such unseemly behaviour and I shall clear the court and charge you all with contempt."

Those present knew better than to cross Judge Jenkins.

The Clerk, sensing a chance to restore his authority spoke. "All rise for Judge Jenkins."

Obediently the court rose. Not a sound was heard above the shuffling of feet on the cramped courtroom floor.

"Be seated." The Judge adjusted his gown and took his place at the centre of proceedings. He turned to the Prosecuting Counsel. "Please state your case."

"The Crown versus John Carter. A charge has been brought that on the night of 27th September, 1763, he did organise and take part in a raid on a warehouse in Penzance with the object of securing a cargo of goods which he claimed had been unfairly removed from his premises. In so doing he did attack and kill, Thomas Chymander of the Parish of St Just in Penwith, who was on guard duty that night. He is therefore charged with murder."

The Judge peered at John over his half-moon spectacles. "How do you plead?"

John drew himself up to his full height and spoke in a calm, resonant voice. "Not guilty on the charge of murder but guilty to the charge of entering the warehouse."

The lawyer for the prosecution was an elderly man well versed in the practise of law. He continued his preamble for twenty minutes, relating to the court the details of the case against John Carter. He paused every now and then to mop his brow with a blue silk neckerchief that dangled loosely from his waistcoat pocket. The court remained spellbound as they learned some of the exploits of the King of Prussia. They were necessary revelations for the Prosecution but they also enhanced his standing with the members of the gallery who were not well versed in the finer points of the law. The wily lawyer knew that romantic gestures were wasted on Judge Jenkins, the facts were the only things of importance in his eyes.

Jan listened intently, every now and then glancing over to where John sat. Early on in the proceedings he had acknowledged Jan's presence with wink and a slight nod of the head but once the Prosecution had started their case, he confined himself to the odd whispered conversation with Mr. Hart and remained expressionless throughout.

Jan searched the sea of faces in the courtroom trying to pick out those he knew. He could see Jake Tanna but any sign of Henry Carter proved fruitless.

"He could have, at least, attended the trial," Jan thought, vaguely irritated at his lack of interest once again.

"Call Sergeant Crowlas to the stand."

Jan stiffened as the Crown Prosecution summoned their first witness.

Mr. Hart was surprised that they had called Sergeant Crowlas so early in the proceedings. Maybe they were so confident of a conviction that they did not deem it necessary to call any other witnesses. He did not know that Peter Pendennis had insisted on Crowlas being the only witness. It would have been foolish to buy too many.

Sergeant Crowlas was an imposing figure as he stood to attention in the witness box. His bright, scarlet uniform showed not a crease or a stain and the brass buttons on his coat shone with elegant splendour. The one blemish was an ugly scar on the side of his face.

The court listened in awe as the booming voice of the Sergeant reverberated off the walls, all present were transfixed by the immensity of the occasion.

Jan could hardly sit still, his nerves twisting at the inside of his stomach. Had he done enough to influence the guardian of the law? He fixed all the powers of his concentration on the man standing a few feet from his seat. Not a flicker of emotion crossed the face of the chief witness for the Prosecution as he answered the questions that were being fired at him in quick succession.

Jan had to admit he was good. In a firm voice, he related his involvement in the case after the warehouse raid. The gallery was warming to him as he portrayed the image of a fine upstanding citizen charged with upholding the letter of the law.

"And tell the Court in your own words what exactly happened to the poor unfortunate Thomas Chyander."

"This is it." Jan caught his breath and moved onto the edge of his seat.

The Sergeant was about to open his mouth when an extraordinary thing happened. The doors at the back of the courtroom were flung open and a man was hurled violently towards the Judge's chair.

There was deathly hush. The man sprawled on the floor tried to get up but was quickly dissuaded by the person following behind.

"Show a little respect for the Judge," said Henry Carter as he gave his victim another push in the back.

The Judge quickly regained his composure. "What is the meaning of this? You are in a court of law."

"Tell the Judge your name," Henry Carter spat at the quivering form of humanity that lay at his feet.

"Thomas Chyander, Your Worship," he stammered.

The Court gasped in amazement. The Judge, who was about to have the court cleared took off his spectacles and peered at the man lying before him.

"Thomas Chyander of the Parish of St. Just in Penwith?"

"Yes, Your Worship, the very same."

The Judge sat looking at the man. This man was supposed to be dead and buried. In all his years at the Bar he had never had to deal with an incidence like this. Finally he addressed the court. "The Court will recess until three o'clock this afternoon."

The atmosphere in the crowded room that had been crackling with tension, suddenly exploded. There was pandemonium, in the history of the Bodmin Assize, there had never been scenes like it. Jan joined the cheering throng, unable to conceal the delight he felt at the timely arrival of Henry Carter. The only two people who remained unmoved throughout were John Carter and the unfortunate Sergeant Crowlas. John, oblivious to the crowded gallery who were chanting his name, was led away by two ushers to await the return of Judge Jenkins.

Jan elbowed his way out of the public gallery. The corridor outside was less crowded but just as incredulous as the sensational news filtered through to those unable to squeeze inside. He was pestered for details by the inquisitive bystanders. He tried to relate what had happened but found it difficult to believe it himself. Fortunately he spotted Mr. Hart in the foyer.

"Ah! Mr. Pendray," he greeted Jan warmly. "I do believe we have won the first battle if not the war."

"They can't hold him now, surely?"

"Not on a charge of murder but remember, Mr. Carter has already pleaded guilty to the charge of entering the warehouse. The Judge will not let that matter pass."

"Is there any chance of speaking with John?"

"None whatsoever I'm afraid. The bailiffs are very touchy about that kind of thing especially after the scenes we have just witnessed in the courtroom. Even I will have difficulty in gaining access and I am his defending counsel."

"Well tell him that I will be here until the end of the trial if he needs me. In the meantime, may I wish you well and good luck."

Jan shook Mr. Hart's hand and left the building. He was glad to breathe in some fresh air. The courtroom had become hot and stuffy with the tangled mass of onlookers so he was happy to walk briskly back to the Hotel.

The bar of the Angel was less crowded than usual and Jan was able to perch himself on one of the stools that were available by the polished cedar counter. He had just ordered a glass of mead when in walked Sergeant Crowlas. Both men froze. The suddenness of the meeting caught both men off guard. Jan was the first to recover.

"Sergeant Crowlas, will you do me the honour of joining me for a drink? I'm sure you need it."

The Sergeant moved forwards uncertainly, the shock of meeting Jan face to face jarring his composure.

"It's most kind of you to offer, Mr. Pendray, but I would sooner drink on my own."

"Come, come, Sergeant, let bygones be bygones, let us celebrate the welcome change of circumstances."

"There is nothing to celebrate."

"That cannot be true. You have just been spared a decision that could have been a burden on your conscience for the rest of your life. If that is not a cause for celebration, I don't know what is."

The confused thoughts that were running through the Sergeant's head were such that he didn't know what to think. Lamely he sat down on the stool next to him. Jan was glad, well aware that the massive Sergeant was capable of picking him up and throwing him horizontally through the window. He sipped the beer that was placed in front of him his massive hand enveloping the glass. Jan almost felt sorry for him.

"You do not know that I would have committed perjury in court," The Sergeant said, sighing heavily.

"True, but I think my paltry act of persuasion and your conscience would be no match against the power of Peter Pendennis."

Sergeant Crowlas winced. "I don't know what you are talking about. Peter Pendennnis means nothing to me."

Jan shrugged and let the matter drop.

"And what about you, Mr. Pendray?" He turned his shoulders towards Jan. "For one so slight in stature you take considerable risks. By rights I should beat the living daylights out of that cocky frame of yours."

Jan grinned.

"It is as well I do not bare any malice," he continued. "Otherwise I would gladly see you fed to the fishes."

He stared hard at Jan who returned it with equal intensity.

"I doubt it, Sergeant. You have too much to lose. I am a minor aberration in your path to the top. It would be a waste of your time as I too, bear no malice and just wish the matter to be forgotten. John Carter has not been found guilty of murder that is all that matters."

With that the two men, realising they had reached an impasse, drained their glasses and went their separate ways. It was to be a long time before their paths crossed again.

Because of his meeting with Sergeant Crowlas, Jan was later than he intended in returning to the Courthouse. He had to settle for a cramped corner of the room where a few people were allowed standing room only. On the dot of three o'clock the court rose for Justice Jenkins. The Judge showed no sign of being affected by the morning session. Dignity was once again restored to the proceedings. He beckoned to those with seats to sit down. Silence reigned, anticipating the words from the guardian of the law.

He spoke slowly and deliberately, measuring his words with a clarity that left no one in any doubt as to who was in charge.

"In view of the extraordinary events this morning, I have no alternative but to declare the verdict on the accused, John Carter, not guilty."

The words were met by a chorus of cheering as the public gallery greeted the verdict with delight.

"But," spat the Judge in such a menacing tone that the rabble were brought to silence, "there is still the case of breaking and entering the warehouse to be considered."

His words were delivered with such venom that the crowd shuffled uncomfortably.

"As this is an unusual case, court etiquette will be waived and I shall summon John Carter to the stand."

It was immediately apparent that the Prosecuting Council and Mr. Hart had spent a large part of their lunchtime in consultation with the Judge.

John Carter was led to the stand and sworn in. The Judge, seeing the accused in front of him asked, "Have you anything to say in mitigation before I pass sentence on your plea of guilty?"

John Carter turned slightly so he could address his remarks to the Judge and those present in the main body of the room.

"Your Honour, I have lived in the County of Cornwall all my life. I have worked for the miners, I have worked on the boats and I have worked on the land. No one has put more into this isolated peninsula than have I, but for what reward? You are surrounded by hard working, proud citizens who work their fingers to the bone for a mere pittance, they strive to earn enough to feed and clothe their families whilst the mine owners, landlords and gentry get fat on their hard earned labours."

A roar of approval arose from the massed ranks in the public gallery.

"I am a simple man, Your Honour," he continued. "I ask for nothing more than a decent living for the common people of Cornwall and if preventing one poor wretch from starving to death is within my means, I will do all that is in my power to help. I have never been accused of causing suffering to those who can ill-afford it and never have I stooped to the despicable level of taking another man's life in cold blood."

Murmurs of approval accompanied by the nodding of heads came from the Gallery.

"Why this case was brought is for you to decide, Your Honour, but if you probe too deeply you may encounter a rottenness in the County that has permeated right to the core of our society."

Roars of approval greeted his words. The Judge was aware of the effect his speech was having on the partisan onlookers, he was well versed in the power of oratory in clouding the real issues at stake. "I must ask you Mr. Carter to keep to the point, political intrigue has no bearing on your plea for mitigation."

John nodded his head respectfully. "I apologise, Your Honour, I will keep to the point. I have admitted to entering the warehouse without authority, of that, I plead guilty."

John paused before continuing. "If, however, it is not a crime to regain one's own property, I plead not guilty and respectfully suggest that those who raided Prussia Cove in the first place should take my place as the accused."

Laughter greeted this remark, its point not lost on a community that paid scant respect to the Excisemen.

"And, in conclusion, I should like to thank those who have worked so hard to clear my name. With them and the people of Cornwall, the King of Prussia rests his defence."

There was second's silence before pandemonium broke out in the Courthouse. The eloquent speech by John Carter had held them spellbound but as soon as he stopped, cheering and chanting swept across the room and into the crowd that had gathered in the street. Grown men, not easily prone to displays of emotion were seen to cry, old ladies waved their sticks in jubilation and many tradesmen clapped their hands in delight.

Jan, too, staggered at the weight of support for his friend, found it difficult to fight back the tears as he found himself caught up in the euphoria of the moment.

Eventually, by the sheer power of his office, Judge Jenkins restored a semblance of order to the proceedings.

"Any more demonstrations and I will clear the court," he snapped. It had the desired effect, silence was established once again.

The Judge, seeing his authority as a guardian of the law had returned, coughed and launched into a long summary of the case. It was listened to with the utmost decorum from those present who were not renowned for their patience over matters of law. The summing up lasted a full thirty minutes, causing a certain amount of shuffling amongst those sitting on the plain wooden benches at the back of the room. Just as this pressure was starting to tell on the back ends of those unfortunates, the Judge moved into the climax of his speech.

"When passing sentence, one must take two things into consideration, firstly, was it an act of malice, contrary to the laws of our land? Secondly, to what extent should the accused be made to pay for his crime? These are the issues I have had to consider when passing judgement."

The Court sat with bated breath.

The Judge turned his attention to John. "Please, rise."

Dutifully the accused rose and stood stiffly to attention.

"John Carter, currently of Prussia Cove in the Parish of Marazion, I find you guilty of unlawfully breaking into a premises with the intention of stealing goods to which you had no rightful claim."

A buzz of anticipation was quickly silenced by a stare from the Judge.

"However," he continued, "I am prepared to accept that you are the rightful owner of the said goods. That, however, does not excuse your blatant breach of the law. I sentence you to twelve months imprisonment to be served in the jail of this town. Case closed."

The Judge gathered up his papers and prepared to leave. The stunned silence that greeted the verdict gave way to jeers. After John's rousing address, they had been confident that he would walk away a free man. They lost no time in showing their disgust.

The Judge, renowned for his iron nerve, was visibly shaken by the hostile reception. He was unused to such ugly scenes in the courtroom and was at a loss on how to deal with it. He never could understand the Cornish. Under the circumstances he thought his verdict was lenient. It was John Carter who saved his embarrassment.

"Friends," he shouted above the uproar. "You have witnessed English justice today. As long as we have Judges of the calibre of the Honourable Henry Jenkins who will not flinch at preserving law and order, you can sleep well in the knowledge that all is not corrupt in our society today. I go to jail willingly to pay for a crime that I foolishly committed."

The roars of disapproval that greeted the verdict, turned to a grudging respect as the public gathering acknowledged the words of John Carter. He was led away to a crescendo of clapping whilst Judge Jenkins slipped surreptitiously out of the door that led to the sanctity of his personal chambers.

"These damned, contrary Cornish," he muttered as he prepared to take his leave of the county as soon as possible.

Jan went in search of Mr. Hart. He needed to talk with a level-headed person, all others around seemed to be losing their reason. He eventually cornered the lawyer as he was making for the privacy of the Council Chambers.

"Mr. Pendray- a fair sentence in the circumstances. Don't you agree?"

"I suppose so," Jan replied. "But you try telling that to the masses of Cornishmen who have come to regard the King of Prussia as a bastion of freedom. They think he is the only one capable of standing up to the corruption that permeates the upper levels of our society."

"Sheer emotion, Mr. Pendray. Very effective in the short term but of little lasting benefit. Inside two weeks John Carter will be forgotten, a mere memory in the hearts of those who worship him today."

"I wonder," Jan mused and then changed the subject. "Is it possible to see John before he begins his sentence?"

"I think that can be arranged, follow me."

Jan entered the chambers and was immediately struck by the plush décor and furnishings that were in stark contrast to the spartan appearance of the public sector of the building.

"Please wait here. " He gestured Jan to a high-backed chair that was not built for comfort. He sat nervously on the edge of the seat feeling uneasy in such impressive surroundings.

He did not have long to wait. A door opened across the room and in walked John Carter. The two men shook hands warmly.

"Jan, how can I ever thank you enough? You have provided me with the finest lawyer in Cornwall who, despite my cussedness, performed miracles in my defence."

Mr. Hart, who had followed his client into the room, smiled wryly. "That's as may be, but I think your brother's intervention saved your life."

"Yes, that was rather dramatic don't you think? Henry has a penchant for style although, I must confess, he left it a shade late. There was no telling which way Sergeant Crowlas was going to turn."

"I wasn't sure either," Jan replied and, with a mischievous grin, went on to tell about the events of the previous night.

John listened with incredulous delight whilst Mr. Hart pretended he did not hear. He did not approve of anything that affected the true course of the law. The three men chatted together for some minutes before the bailiffs politely inquired whether they might be permitted to escort their prisoner to the Governor of Bodmin jail.

"Well, Jan, I will leave you now," John said and grabbed his hand for the last time. "Remember, there is always a welcome for you at Prussia Cove. Perhaps we can continue our acquaintance when I come out?"

Jan nodded vigorously. "I shall be waiting for you."

With that, the two comrades hugged and parted company. Jan turned away to hide a tear that had embarrassingly fallen from his eye.

CHAPTER 12

Jan's journey from Bodmin to Truro was something of a luxury. Mr. Hart had kindly offered him a lift in his hired chaise, a far more civilised form of transport than trusting to the inclemency of the weather on horseback. Neither spoke much on the journey, feeling a sense of anti-climax after the excitement of the day. Jan was glad as it gave him a chance to ponder over what he was going to do with his life in the future. After mulling over the possibilities during the three hour journey, he was no nearer to a solution. He disliked being inactive even though he had enough money to tide him over for a few weeks, but the opportunities all seemed tame after his adventures with John Carter.

It was Mr. Hart who broke the silence as the chaise clattered down the hill into Truro.

"Will you have a bite of supper with me, Mr. Pendray? It will break your journey to Falmouth."

Jan readily agreed, he was not looking forward to the lonely ride back to Falmouth on a chilly autumn evening. They eventually shook to a halt on the cobbled stones outside the Red Lion. It was dark and the blast of warmth from the giant fireplace that greeted them in the back lounge was a welcome relief to the weary travellers. Mr. Hart was well known by the staff and in an instant a tray of food was placed in front of them. As they were eating, three men entered the lounge and stood talking amongst themselves. It was not difficult to gather the gist of their conversation.

"So Carter got one year," said one.

"Ruffian, should be hanged," said another.

"It was only an impassioned speech that saved him apparently. There's no doubt the man was guilty."

The hackles on Jan's neck began to rise. Mr. Hart, aware of his temper, hastily suppressed the impulsiveness of his companion. ""Hush, Mr. Pendray," he said as Jan's fist came crashing down on the table. "You cannot stop people talking-you must accept that. In their eyes John Carter was guilty whatever the verdict."

Jan returned to his food but kept staring at the little gathering which were blocking the heat from the fire.

"Who are they?" He asked.

"The one on the left is Sir Roderick Boscowan, the second Viscount of Falmouth, one of the richest landowners in Cornwall. The one seated on the stool is Sir James St.Aubyne, self- styled champion of the Cornish tinners – straight as a dye that one, inherited his father's temperament so they say. Even the Prime Minister, Mr. Walpole is reputed to have said of his father, that all men have their price except St. Aubyne."

"And what of the other?" Jan was glaring at the man who had uttered the remarks about John Carter.

"Ah, now that is Sir Thomas Pendarves, he owns half of the mining interests in Camborne and Redruth. Reputedly his obsession with Copper is such that he has been known to mix punch in a coffin made from the stuff and serve it as an aperitif to his house guests. A hard taskmaster by all accounts."

Jan had taken an instant dislike to the fellow although he was prepared to tolerate the other two. If the stories were true, he had heard that Sir Roderick and Sir James St. Aubyne were, at least, doing something to improve the conditions of the Cornish miners, even if that was pitifully small.

They finished their meal in silence and the three gentry quickly moved on to more mundane topics such as the price of Copper on the open market. The matter of John Carter was dismissed as quickly as it had arisen. Mr. Hart paid the bill and they got up to leave. Jan, however, could not let the matter rest. The remark about his friend was smouldering away in a fire of injustice. He could not let the blackening of John Carter's name pass by without comment. As he went out of the dining room he turned to the three men and said, "John Carter was not guilty of murder as the trial proved. I witnessed the trial and I would thank you, sir, not to make such slanderous comments about which you know nothing."

Without waiting for a reply, he strode out of the room leaving the three men with their mouths hanging open at such a rude interruption to their conversation. Mr. Hart had left hurriedly when he saw what Jan was about to do but he permitted himself a smile once he reached the pavement outside the Red Lion. He hoped that Sir Thomas would not penalise his business because of his associate.

Jan wasted no time in thanking Mr. Hart for his meal and all that he had done for his client, before he saddling up and climbing the steep hill out of town. Pushing the poor horse to its limits, he was in Falmouth in just over an hour. A further ten minutes he was nestling down in the comfort of milk-white sheets and feeling the warmth of Meg as she snuggled down beside him. It was good to be home.

Jan spent the next two weeks in blissful relaxation enjoying the comforts Meg showered upon him and repaying her by taking a turn behind the bar in the evenings.

Jan had become something of a celebrity since the trial. Word had leaked out about his involvement in the raid and his subsequent swim across Mount's Bay. The Falmouth Advertiser had run a lengthy article on him and he was pleased that the publicity he gained resulted in more customers frequenting the Ship and Castle. Previously, Meg's trade had not risen above the odd tradesman and a few sailors who happened to be in port. Now it was not uncommon to see the occasional gentleman drop in, hoping that he might set eyes on the infamous Jan Pendray. Jan kept a modest profile on such occasions, politely answering questions put to him but never divulging the background to the case.

After a couple of weeks of gracious living he became restless and bored. He could not complain about his circumstances, Meg was too kind by half and he had no right to feel unhappy with his lot. It was just that he could see himself slipping into a very pleasant existence which, he feared, could be with him for the rest of his life. He was too young to settle down. Meg was aware of his restlessness but was powerless to help- it was something he would have to work out for himself.

It was in this mood of aimless drifting that Jan sat behind the bar one evening in November. His deliberations were cut short by the Inn door opening and in walked Sir James Aubyne. He was alone. Jan recognised him instantly, more from the crop of grey hair that protruded from underneath an expensive looking cap, than the refined cut of his flamboyant clothes. Recognition came slowly to St. Aubyne, he knew he had seen Jan somewhere before but he couldn't fathom out where.

"Good evening to you, Sir," said Jan politely. "It is a pleasure to have the company of such an astute and able gentleman in the Ship and Castle."

Sir James acknowledged the compliment and ordered a bottle of the best Claret that Meg kept on the top shelf but never sold.

"Would you care to join me young man," he said. "It would be a waste to drink such fine wine on my own."

Sir James winked before adding, "too good to be from normal channels, I'll be bound."

Jan ignored the last remark and placed two glasses on the bar in front of them.

"I must apologise for my behaviour in the Red Lion, sir, it was not meant to be a slight on your character, more rashness on my part when your companion made disparaging remarks about John Carter."

Realisation dawned on Sir James, he remembered now, the brash young man with fiery intensity in his eyes.

"I was too impulsive," Jan continued. "I had just come from the trial and witnessed first hand, the best of English justice."

Sir James St. Aubyne shrugged his shoulders. "It is of no consequence. I find Sir Thomas quite nauseating myself at times, he belongs to that group of people who feel they have an enduring right to state their views on any subject under the sun and expect to find others in total agreement."

Jan smiled, relieved that his outburst had not caused offence.

"May I enquire why such an influential gentleman should choose to drink in the Ship and Castle?"

"I came to see this Jan Pendray that everybody from Lanhydrock to St. Michael's Mount is talking about. I take it, young sir, that you are the person I seek?"

Jan saw little point in denying it and nodded his head slowly.

"Yes, but I don't make a song and dance about it. To tell you the truth, I find all this fuss bewildering. I only encourage it for the sake of the trade it has brought to the Ship and Castle."

"Commendable, men should always use whatever talents they have in order to extricate themselves and their families from the interminable rigours of poverty."

He sipped carefully at the glass of claret and let it linger in his throat before continuing,

"There are thousands of miners in Camborne and Redruth who would give their right arm for a chance to pull themselves out of the everlasting struggle to provide enough food and warmth to see out the winter. Sadly, a number will die in the process."

"I hear that you have a lot to do with the mining community, sir?"

James St. Aubyne's face turned grey and, for the first time, Jan noticed that he was talking with a man of advancing years.

"Yes," he sighed, "I have a lot to do with the miners. I fear, not as much as I would like."

"They tell me life is not good in Camborne and Redruth with the onset of winter."

"You have no comprehension of what these poor devils have to put up with, a pittance for a wage and working conditions that are abhorrent to any decent human being. Small wonder that the majority of them seek solace in the gin shops and Kiddlewinks, it is the only way they know how to forget the hellish conditions they have to face when they return underground."

They both sat contemplating the enormity of the problem.

"Can you take me there?" Jan asked suddenly.

St. Aubyne eyed him curiously and seemed to be mulling over the strange request.

"I'll take you there, Jan Pendray and I will show you to what depths man has sunk in this part of the country."

An edge of authority had crept into his tone. Jan had nothing but respect, here was a man of Christian principles and an iron will whose determination to fight for the rights of the miner were etched into his soul.

An hour later, Sir James St. Aubyne left the Ship and Castle. He was more than a little excited, he had seen in Jan, the very qualities he needed. It only required some subtle channelling and his objective would be partially achieved.

That evening Meg could see a strange, new force acting within Jan. There was a spring in his step and a solid purpose in the most menial of tasks. She was glad. She had become tired of Jan's lethargy and restlessness. Lately he was not the same person who had so captivated her when they first met. He needed a cause or a sound objective if he was to ignite those around him, without John Carter he had become stale and demotivated.

Jan left on horseback the following morning leaving a glowing Meg still high from the lovemaking of the previous night. He felt a tinge of excitement as his horse trotted along the gentle incline away from the port and onto the granite outcrops in the distance. Soon the dense greenery of the Falmouth estuary gave way to open moorland. Dotted with increasing frequency, were massive granite boulders and the occasional mine stack belching forth thick, black smoke heralding the approach to one of the most densely populated areas in the country.

By eleven o'clock the sun had emerged from a watery sky but the wind that always blew on the moor, was keen enough to make Jan sink deep into his fleece-lined riding jacket. The mist that still swirled around the bleak and austere outcrop of Carnmarth was the highest point in this part of Cornwall. Jan kept it to his left and descended gently into the village of Lanner, a tiny community of a few houses huddled in the lee of Carnmenellis. No sooner had he reached the village, he was on the way up again, his horse sweating profusely as he gallantly strove to climb another interminable hill.

Once at the top, the mist had lifted giving a view that made Jan gasp. He had no idea such a vista could be found in Cornwall. Stretched out before him were the twin mining communities of Camborne and Redruth. Hundred upon hundred of mine stacks pointed to the sky, belching forth spirals of thick, black smoke. Every so often a gap would appear in the sky and a glimpse of the silvery sea could be seen as it pounded on the rocky shoreline eight miles in the distance.

It held a grim fascination for Jan who had never experienced anything but green fields and the open sea, here was the legacy of wealth and profit that lined the pockets of the fortunate landowners. The desecration of the land was the price that had to be paid. Jan scanned the landscape but could not see a single tree apart from the thin veil of green that surrounded the Basset Estate at Tehidy. The smoking chimneys dominated the land with odd patches of grassland that belonged to the miner-farmers providing the only colour in a vista of brown and grey.

Jan stood for a long time staring, he could see the relevance of the industrial landscape but was loathe to admit it. The mines here provided more work than anywhere else in Europe, without them the local population would starve. Eventually, he remounted and headed for Redruth. He took an instant dislike to the rows of tiny houses, cramped together with tight, narrow streets, he was a country boy at heart and found towns claustrophobic. He shuddered as he passed by the first of the granite houses. Thank goodness, fate had decreed that he should not be born in such squalid surroundings. But it was the people that caused him the greatest concern. Sadness and poverty showed on every face. The children, sitting listlessly on the steps of their homes, eyes sunken and the skin stretched tight across their thin faces. The women, proud and defiant did their best to smile but Jan could see the weight of concern hanging heavy on their shoulders. The pock-marked faces of the men, sallow with fatigue, gave hints of the kind of life they had to lead in order to feed and clothe their families. Jan was shocked, at least sea-faring men could survive on the fruits of the sea. Here malnutrition seeped from every pore. And yet, as Jan looked around him, he was aware of a fierce pride burning just below the surface. The doorsteps were scrubbed spotless and the feeling of togetherness blazed forth. It was this mining camaraderie that saw suffering shared, providing an introverted existence that bore no great love for the world outside.

Jan sensed the resentment as he reigned in his horse outside the London Inn. Small groups of men who stood on the street corners and alleyways stopped and stared as he dismounted. To them a horse spelt money, a symbol of wealth way beyond the pockets of the average miner. No one spoke, content to stare and envy the young master who dared to ride into their town.

Jan tethered his horse to the watering place outside the Inn and quickly went inside glad to be away from those sad and hostile eyes.

Sir James St. Aubyne was waiting for him in the snug. He was quick to see Jan's uneasiness.

"They won't harm you or your horse," he said reassuringly. "They rarely see a horse or a man with such a fine riding jacket and when they do, it is on the back of a mine owner or Adventurer for whom they work."

Jan sat down next to Sir James and sipped gratefully as a glass of hot mead was placed in front of him.

"Poor devils," he muttered, "and to think I used to complain if we went one week with only mackerel for dinner. Some of those men look as if they haven't eaten fish for ages."

"They most probably haven't, my boy, it's a sad and unenviable life being a miner these days."

For the next hour they chatted about mining, Jan, anxious to learn, but afraid to ask too many questions in deference to his distinguished companion.

"Well, Jan, how would you like to go down a mine?" It was a statement rather than question and, before he had time to think, he was whisked out of the Inn and into a chaise that had been prepared outside. Sir James issued an order to the ostler to have Jan's horse ready for their return before sunset and they were off. Sir James took the reins and steered the horse-drawn carriage up the street and on towards Gwennap.

Jan had heard of Gwennap from Henry Carter, an area thickly populated with mines and a favourite gathering place for preachers of the Methodist faith. The raw and uncouth miners generally preferred the sanctity of the gin shops to the hell raising orators who spoke nothing but fire and brimstone and eternal damnation to those of lesser persuasion. Most thought they were one step from hell underground anyway and did not care to be reminded when they reached clean air.

After climbing steadily for some minutes in which they passed many groups of weary miners as they filed away from the morning shift, the land levelled out. Once again Jan was confronted by the mass of smoking chimneys as they kept the pumps working underground. To Jan it was impressive and depressing at the same time. He had little knowledge of mining and found it difficult to appreciate the enormity of the problems the men had to face when they went underground. It was evident from the sullen looks and open resentment on the faces of the miners that they had scant regard for the two men in the elegant chaise.

Sir James sensed his companion's unease and smiled.

"They are a fickle lot, these miners, one moment they are after your blood simply because you are fortunate enough to have money, the next they are moved to tears by a wizened old man like John Wesley, a preacher who extols the virtue of godliness and friendship."

"Do they really believe in John Wesley?" Jan had heard of him but nothing more.

"John Wesley is like a saint to the Cornish miner. He brings a ray of light into their dull lives. Although he is past his prime these days, he is still able to command a large audience wherever he speaks. It is said that back in the thirties he preached to 30,000 at Gwennap Pit turning a mob of hysterical miners into a congregation as quiet as lambs."

Jan nodded in agreement. "I know what you mean. We get the occasional miner in the Ship and Castle but they keep themselves to themselves and trying to start a conversation is virtually impossible."

"Almost, but not quite," replied the ageing Lord. "Wesley managed it."

Another group of weary men trudged past as the chaise descended into a small valley containing three stacks, all belching the eternal column of smoke.

"Welcome to Wheal Cupid," said Sir James as he reigned in the chaise opposite the first of the pump houses.

Jan was glad to get out and stretch his legs, it was a constant source of irritation that he could withstand the meanest of seas but he could not adjust to travelling comfortably on land. The arrival of the chaise had sparked a hive of activity led by the Mine Captain who stood waiting by the engine house.

"Good day to 'ee, sir, "he boomed . "There's a fair amount coming out of the main lode at present, four feet wide in places. Those two tributers we took on last week have found a secondary lode. It's only eighteen inches but it could open out."

"Good news, Treventon." Sir James was obviously delighted. "How are the two young boys working out?"

Treventon shrugged his shoulders and grinned. "They'll be alright, sir, don't 'ee fret, I'll see to that. Their four pence a week is a fortune compared with what they've been used to."

Jan observed the Mine Captain with interest. He was a rarity in Cornwall, a six foot giant with broad shoulders and huge forearms to match. He had never seen such a powerfully built man before. It was little wonder that he had risen to such an eminently respectable position.

"Treventon, I want you to meet an acquaintance of mine, Jan Pendray, you may have heard about him."

Jan stepped forward and shook hands with the big man.

"Aye, I've heard of you, Jan Pendray. Welcome to Wheal Cupid. Not quite the size of Wheal Virgin or Ting-Tang but still a happy mine with the rare distinction of having an owner who cares about his men."

"I'm pleased to make your acquaintance, Mr. Treventon. Sir James has kindly offered a guided tour of the area and maybe a trip underground."

The Mine Captain roared with laughter.

"You sure you want to go below? A lot down there would do anything to get out if they could."

Jan grinned. "I've never been one for shrinking away from adversity, Mr. Treventon."

"Follow me, then," he said, still laughing. They walked towards a small door on the side of a block of wooden sheds whilst leaving Sir James free to review the fruits of his business enterprise.

Inside the hut, Jonas Treventon handed Jan one of the blue overalls that hung on pegs by the window.

"Put this on, you'll need it if you want to keep the dust away from your clothes."

Jan donned the overall and felt a small schism of anticipation as the Mine Captain lit one of the Davey safety lamps that stood in the corner.

"One of the finest inventions ever made, these lamps," the Captain commented. "A long way from the candle and wick that we used in the old days."

With the lamp lit, Jonas Treventon led them down a short corridor connecting two of the huts. Jan could see the dark stains on the bare timber walls, the result of a multitude of grimy hands as the miners reappeared after a gruelling day in the bowels of the earth.

"Like rats from a hole," thought Jan as he imagined a chain of men emerging from the countless holes in the ground at the end of each shift. It was a curious sensation, he shuddered at the idea of burrowing thousands of feet below the surface but at the same time he was jealous of the camaraderie that seemed to exist amongst the men.

Jonas Treventon opened the door at the end of the corridor and beckoned Jan through. He found himself in a tiny compartment with barely enough room to stand. He started to tremble. No more than a foot away was a gaping hole of total darkness. He was standing at the entrance to the mine. He was gripped by a peculiar desire to run. The black hole filled him with a chilling sense of panic.

The Captain read his thoughts and grinned.

"Aye, it catches you like that the first time, some never get used to it."

Jan took a deep breath and braced himself for what was to follow.

"Lead on, Captain, I'll follow but I am not saying I shall enjoy it."

Captain Treventon threw back his head and roared with laughter, the resonant sound echoing of the walls of the shaft until it was lost somewhere far below.

Wheal Cupid was not large enough to warrant a cage for transporting miners to the lode face, the only means of descent was by an iron ladder on the side of the shaft. In extreme cases it was possible to ride up on the winch which was used for hauling up the ore but as the Mine Captain pointed out, it took much longer and was not without risk.

The first rungs of the ladder were easy enough and Jan found his confidence restored, his legs stopped shaking and he was able to descend easily into the abyss. After what seemed an interminable time, during which Jan watched the glimmer of light from the shaft entrance slowly disappear to the merest speck in a blanket of darkness, he felt his feet touch solid rock. Captain Treventon was waiting for him lamp in hand. They were standing in a large cavern, with two tunnels bearing off to the left and right. Jan could see rivulets of water splashing down the walls, glistening in the glow of the Davey lamp. The steady trickle of water was the only sound to break the silence. Jan was extremely grateful that he had the big Mine Captain as his guide. This was a truly inhospitable place.

They took the left hand tunnel out of the cavern, walking at such a brisk pace that Jan found it difficult to keep up. The shaft shelved gently downhill until they reached a depth of five fathoms. Jan became aware of the acrid smell of sulphur. It was so strong that he was forced to cover his face with a sweat-stained neckerchief he found in the overalls he was wearing.

After walking for twenty minutes, Jan was again seized by an inexplicable sense of panic. For all he knew he was entering the chambers of the Devil, it was only the comforting shoulders of the Mine Captain that gave him courage to continue.

At last they stopped. Above the sound of their own heavy breathing they could hear the distinct sounds of metal on stone. An occasional voice told they were near the lode face. The sound of voices was comforting to Jan. At least he was not on his own. The deeper he went, the more he began to understand the Cornish miner and their tight-knit community.

The last part of the descent was truly hair-raising. On their hands and knees they had to crawl through a narrow tunnel and then climb down a single rope with no protection from a fifty foot drop should the climber be careless enough to lose his grip.

Jan was drained both mentally and physically. The Mine Captain cast his lamp over the slumped form of his companion and laughed once again. He was joined by the men from the lode face as they crowded around to ridicule the unfortunate stranger. Jan grinned feebly, taking the ribbing in good part. This was their land and he felt like an intruder.

Jonas Treventon melted into the gloom for a while, leaving Jan to reflect on his experience. He was in a large gallery that stretched up for a hundred feet on either side. All the way up he could see the glow of candles providing just enough light for the fifty or so miners to hack away at the four lodes that were being worked. It was a touching sight, each man isolated in his own pool of light but also, a member of a highly skilled team. One false move by one of the team and the whole edifice could come crumbling down. From somewhere above a voice started to sing. A mellow, sonorous sound that reverberated about the gallery. The tune was taken up by the others until the whole space was alive with the sound of song.

The perfection of the choir and the location of the performance brought tears to Jan's eyes. He forgot about his aching muscles and was swept away by the occasion that would have graced the most regal cathedral in the land.

The singing died away as quickly as it had begun and it was back to the chink, chink of the stopes and the squeal of the winch as it hauled the ore to the surface.

Captain Treventon returned. "Some fine singing in this mine, Jan, don't 'ee think?"

"They sing like skylarks. Where do they get the strength?"

"You get used to it after a while, it's not paradise I'll admit but there are plenty worse off. In some mines the only way up and down is by the main shaft. If you're not hit by falling ore, you're likely to be dashed to pieces by the swinging buckets as they go past."

Jan shuddered and changed the subject. "Do you have much trouble with water in this mine?"

"Not as bad as some, we are working shallow here. Some of the lower adits have been known to flood. Sir James is talking about a new pump so we can go deeper, then we might have problems."

"Would that be the new Boulton and Watt mine engine that he is after?"

The Mine Captain peered at Jan with respect.

"That's the one, Jan, you know of 'n?"

"Only what is written in the broadsheets, all the new mines seem to be having them."

"Not all, Jan, not all. We're lucky to have a boss who cares about the safety of his men. Some don't give a bugger just as long as the ore gets to the surface. There are owners who don't care if they lose a few men or let their workers toil in waste deep water."

Jan could see the injustice of an exploited workforce. "Why don't the miners do something about it?"

"What can they do? The mine owners control their lives. If they protest, they are out of a job. 15 shillings a week is better than bugger all, which is what you would get down here at this time of year. Don't get me wrong, the miners will work willingly as long as they can earn enough to feed and clothe their families. Unfortunately not all of them do."

Jan could feel the familiar fire rise in his belly. "I think it's a scandal that men of wealth and influence should allow this to happen. It would not take too much of their fat incomes to solve the problem."

Jonas Treventon eyed the boy next to him quizzically, he had heard stories about him which he had taken with a pinch of salt, watching him now, he wasn't so sure. There was a fire burning in him, perhaps he really did swim across Mount's Bay. Secretly he had been impressed by Jan's efforts underground but he was wary, there was an impulsiveness about the boy that could either drive him to great things or consign him to the end of a rope. He smiled to himself in the dark and stroked his chin.

Jan spent over an hour at the hub of the mine, watching the men work and fondling the pit ponies as they wheeled the precious ore to the surface. His fear of being underground eased as he adjusted to the oppressive heat and the total darkness but he was still wary of the dangers away from the comforting glow of the candles and lanterns.

The journey back to grass was more arduous as it was uphill but the knowledge that every step took him closer to the surface was ample compensation. The constant dripping of water was a stimulant rather than a hazard and Jan welcomed the cooling effect it had on his perspiring body. Nonetheless, he was glad to see the pinpoint of light grow gradually bigger as he climbed the ladder for the last time. Jonas Treventon was waiting for him at the top of the shaft.

"Well done, Jan, how did you like your first trip below ground?"

Jan grinned ruefully. "It was an experience, I'll say that, but to say I enjoyed it would be a lie. To do that every day for a pittance would drive me to drink. Small wonder the Kiddlewinks in Redruth do such a roaring trade."

Jonas Treventon grinned and ushered Jan into a small cubicle where he found a jug of warm water and a towel.

"The boss is thinking of installing running water at the pithead for the men but it is difficult to get enough pressure to pump the water out to here. It would be the first mine in the county if he did."

"Is there enough copper down there to keep the mine going?" Jan enquired as he let the tepid water run down over his grimy body.

"You can never be sure. Sometimes a lode will open out to two feet and then suddenly finish, just like that. You'll never find 'n again. The ore's good quality from this mine so I reckon it's worth keeping open."

"Where does the ore go from here?"

"Bissoe- on trucks, then 'tis loaded onto barges and shipped down to Falmouth. You've probably seen the lighters in the bay. They're too big to get up the river."

Jan nodded. "Aye, I've seen them. I've often wondered why they can't smelt the ore in Cornwall. It seems a lot of the mine profit goes with those boats."

"Too expensive, there are not enough trees in Cornwall to fire the smelting works and coal would have to be brought from Bristol and Wales. There was some talk of the Basset family bringing coal to Portreath but nothing came of it. You're right, of course, if we could smelt here it would make a big difference especially as there is tin lying down there doing nothing."

They dried off briskly as the chill of the evening contrasted greatly with the heat generated fifty feet below. Sir James was waiting for them as they emerged from the hut.

"A good day, Jan, I trust?"

"Yes, thankyou, sir. An experience I would not have missed. Now I know what it is like to burrow deep into the earth."

"Well, we best be getting back before it is too dark."

Jan turned to the Mine Captain.

"Thankyou Jonas, it was a privilege to see your mine, it is a pity they are not all as well run as yours. I hope we can meet again sometime."

Jonas Treventon beamed. "A real pleasure Jan Pendray, I am sure we will see each other again."

With that he winked at Sir James and made off towards the pump house.

The journey back to Redruth was uneventful. The two men chatted idly about various aspects of mining of which Jan had no knowledge until they reached the door of the Red Lion. Both men were ravenous so Jan eagerly accepted the offer to dine with Sir James.

It was past nine o'clock when Jan saddled up and guided his horse back up the hill to Lanner. By now the gin shops were spilling their customers onto the street and Jan was glad to leave the town behind him. Drunken miners were not renowned for their decorum and he was acutely aware of the figure he cut as he spurred the horse on as quickly as he dared.

Once away from the crowds darkness enveloped him like a blanket. He was glad, he never considered himself to be a cut above the miners but it was obvious they envied his position. True, he had had the rudiments of an education. He thanked his father for that. Otherwise he felt no different. It was the desperation caused by hunger that drove these people to resentment and frustration. Jan shuddered at the thought of what might happen should they unite behind a common voice.

Jan let the horse guide him home. He could see nothing, the clouds obscured the moon and there were no other riders to share his progress. Winter nights in Cornwall did not encourage nocturnal travellers.

Meg had waited up. He was grateful, he was chilled to the bone and he was thirsty. For the first time in his life he was beginning to appreciate the benefits of having a woman who cared. The customers had long since departed but Meg had stirred the dying embers of the fire in the back room and a welcome blast of heat greeted him as he sprawled out on the mat in front of the hearth. She brought in a steaming mug of chocolate and handed it to him. He took it gratefully and let the steam rise in front of his face. Meg sat beside him, her black curls tumbling over her shoulders. She said nothing, comfortable with the silence.

It was Jan who broke the spell. "We don't know how lucky we are. Those poor devils have to work in some of the most appalling conditions I have ever seen and for what? Fifteen measily shillings a week. Meanwhile the mine owners get fat on the proceeds. It's not fair."

"Even Sir James Aubyne?"

"No, Meg, not him. He is a rarity. He is a man who has vision enough to know that caring for his workforce is the best way to see that he gets the maximum from the mine. Not that he is entirely free from blame. He must share some of the responsibility for keeping the miners' wages at such a paltry level."

"It's hardly his fault. He keeps his own workforce happy he can't be expected to carry all the injustices on his shoulders."

Jan stared grimly at the flames shooting up the chimney. "Sooner or later they'll all have to take notice. If you could have seen the look on the faces of those starving miners I saw today...."

His voice trailed off. Meg saw the dangerous look in his eyes and knew how shocked he had been.

"A miner will put up with bad working conditions," he continued, "but when a seven hour shift, six days a week will not provide enough food for his family, then God knows what will happen. One spark and fifty thousand people may not be responsible for their actions."

He drained his cup and placed it on the hearth. The dim light from the fading fire cast a shadow across Meg's face. Jan saw the glow from her cheeks and touched the soft skin around the nape of her neck. Gently he pulled back the locks of black hair and kissed her shoulder. She snuggled closer trying to control the desire that was growing inside her. She smiled inwardly, if only he knew the power of his touch. But Jan, too, was unable to suppress the physical need that was rising like a minestack within him.

"Meg, I need you, "he whispered softly and with a swift movement he picked her up and carried her up the narrow panelled staircase.

CHAPTER 13

For the rest of the week Jan could not get mining out of his head. He took long walks along the waterfront and gazed out to the lighters in the bay with a new-found respect. He watched the flat-bottomed barges creep down the River Fal and into the bay. He had become acutely aware of the problems the ordinary working man both above the ground and below. John Carter had a lot to do with it. Thanks to his generosity, Jan was able to live a comfortable life without having to resort to the sweat and toil that was the lot of most Cornishmen. For the first time he understood what Sergeant Crowlas had gone through. In a nutshell, Jan had a conscience. It seemed unjust that he should be enjoying life whilst vast numbers were working their hands to the bone for 15 shillings a week. He did not dwell on it long, after all, what could he do about it? The solution lay with those in power.

It was in this confused state of mind that Jan wandered into Pegotties, a coffee hall on the Falmouth waterfront. He was a regular customer, not because he particularly liked the clientele but because it afforded a magnificent view across the Harbour towards the tiny fishing village of Flushing. It was a nostalgic stretch of water. He had grown up on it. Many was the time he had cut afternoon school on the pretext of a headache and gone rushing down to the small dinghy he had moored by the harbour steps. Sometimes his father caught him and showed him the back of his hand but it was worth it, the excitement of the sea lapping against the side of the boat and the rush of adrenaline when he hooked mackerel on his makeshift line, was worth the pain.

Jan smiled inwardly as he remembered with affection the concern his father showed. He knew his anger would not last long and, if he could catch a few fish, he would be back in favour in no time. He missed his father more than he cared to admit.

The coffee hall was half-empty so Jan had no difficulty securing a booth overlooking the water. No sooner had he settled into his seat than the door opened and in walked Peter Pendennis. On his arm was Anna.

There was no avoiding the confrontation, both of them recognised Jan at the same time. Peter Pendennis was caught off guard momentarily but recovered quickly.

"Mr. Pendray, how very nice to see you," he said smoothly, offering Jan his hand.

Jan was caught in two minds, whether to land his fist on Pendennis's chin or to leave his coffee and get out as soon as possible. In fact he did neither, shaking the proffered hand and inviting them to join him.

Anna was radiant. Her cheeks were flushed from the wind but this added to her beauty. She gave Jan a dazzling smile that caused Jan's heart to pound in a manner that took him back to the happy days before their unfortunate parting.

He bowed and asked softly. "How are you, Anna?"

"Very well, thank you, Jan and you? I hear you are an important man these days."

"I am well also, but I think you exaggerate my importance. Don't believe all you hear."

"Come now, Sir, you are too modest." Peter Pendennnis interrupted. "To swim across Mount's Bay is no mean achievement. Nor is the loyalty you have shown to such an honoured thief as the King of Prussia."

Jan bristled but ignored the remark. "I have been sitting here thinking about the past. When we were at school together, this was our stretch of water. Do you remember?"

Pendennis hesitated for a moment before replying.

"Yes, I remember, it seems a long time ago when Miss Trenerry tried to teach us how to spell and add."

Despite themselves they reminisced about their school days. Jan had always had a crush on Anna and she liked Jan but it was Peter Pendennis who was always trying to come between them. He never let Jan forget the superiority of his station.

"I hear that you are getting married, may I offer you my congratulations. Have you fixed a date?"

Anna cast an anxious glance at her betrothed. "It is true but we have not finalised the day. Peter would get married tomorrow but I have my father to consider, he is getting old and needs me to look after him."

Peter Pendennis cast his eyes upwards. "I have told you, my dear, all you have to do is sell that hovel you are living in and both you and your father can move into Pendennis castle."

"It is not as simple as that Peter. Father is very fond of Merryn, it would break his heart to leave."

Pendennis shrugged his shoulders and let the matter rest.

Anna turned to Jan. "What are your plans for the future, Jan?"

"I'm not sure, at the moment. Maybe I'll sign up with the Navy. They will be taking on hands soon. War with France cannot be far away. Or perhaps I will wait until John Carter is released and go to America. He has friends out there who reckon there are fortunes to be made for those prepared to take the risk."

Peter Pendennis could not let the comment pass. "John Carter is lucky to be alive."

"And what makes you say that?" Jan asked coolly.

"The man is a murderer, no doubt about it. Anna and I were astonished that he got off so lightly, weren't we dear?"

Anna blushed but did not answer the question while Jan clenched his fist under the table. How could he sit there and tell such a bare-faced lie especially as he was implicated in the whole saga.

Anna knew Jan too well as she recognised the symptoms of old.

"I'm sure we do not want to talk about the past, do we?" She said hurriedly.

"Like hell we don't," blazed Jan, unable to control himself any longer. "John Carter was innocent and if it were not for the arrival of his brother in court, he would have been hanging from the gallows, all because someone was trying to frame him. I wonder who was behind that?"

He spat the question at Pendennis with such venom that Anna could not suppress a cry. Pendennis remained motionless his face giving nothing away. He continued smoothly,

"In that case I apologise, sir, I am evidently not aware of the background to the case. I have merely formulated my opinion from those of others."

"Like Sergeant Crowlas?"

Pendennis remained impassive. "Who is Sergeant Crowlas?"

Jan sat back and relaxed a malicious smile crossing his face. He had heard all he wanted. Pendennis may not have shown anything on the inscrutable face of his but Jan knew he was lying, he had seen them together in Bodmin. It was only for Anna's sake that Jan did not labour the point. She was mystified by the heightening of tension caused by the mention of John Carter.

Jan finished his coffee swiftly and got up to leave.

"May I wish you both, every happiness in the future," he said stiffly.

"Thankyou, Jan," Anna replied softly. "I shall cherish those words as they have come from you."

There was no mistaking the tenderness in her voice and Jan felt an overwhelming desire to sweep her in his arms and tell her she was making the biggest mistake of her life. However, he choked back his emotion and left.

The chance encounter upset him, more than he cared to admit. He thought that his feelings for Anna had been locked away for ever, it was not the case. His heart raced at the mention of her name, he could not understand it He never felt like that with other women.

Meg could sense something had happened when he returned to the Ship and Castle but she made no comment. He took a bottle of mead off the shelf and proceeded to drink himself into a stupor. It wasn't only Anna, but also, the issue of what was he going to do with his life? Boredom and routine were beginning to play on his nerves, the visit to the mine, providing only a brief respite from the listlessness that seemed to be affecting his every move.

When he could no longer sit on the chair he allowed Meg to drag him upstairs to the bedroom where he could sleep it off.

He awoke at five. His head felt as though it had been kicked by a mule and his mouth was as parched as a baker's oven. He groaned heavily as he tried to lift his head, finding the weight too much, he slumped back on the pillow. He was disgusted with himself. He disliked excessive drinking and frequently ejected men from the Inn who had over imbibed. He regarded it as a weakness of character if a man had to rely on drink to face the realities of life. Consequently he was full of remorse for his errant behaviour.

When he managed to struggle to a sitting position, Meg came in with a steaming mug of tea.

"The cure for all ills," she said brightly. "Especially, excess mead."

Jan took it gratefully, letting the brown liquid lubricate the arid wastes of his throat.

"I'm sorry, Meg," he mumbled, refusing to look at her.

"What's there to be sorry about? It happens all the time in an ale house."

"I feel so stupid when I get drunk and it never solves anything."

Meg stood looking at him. For all his bravado he was engagingly naïve.

"You saw her didn't you?"

"Was it that obvious?"

"It was to me. I remember the last time you saw her."

"I spoke to her, Meg, I actually held a conversation with her and Peter Pendennis."

Meg raised an eyebrow. "And what did he have to say?"

"He's going to marry Anna, they are already betrothed."

Jan drained his mug and sighed.

"I must look awful," he sighed fingering the stubble on his chin and making a perfunctory gesture at wiping the sleep from his eyes. "I think I will go out for a walk let the sea brush away the cobwebs."

Meg smiled and left him to it.

The sharpness of the evening air took his breath away as he left the warm comfort of the snug and plunged into the night. The onset of darkness and the gentle swirl of misty rain meant that all but the hardiest street vendors had made tracks for home. Jan pulled his collar up and trudged off in the direction of the Moor. Soon he was out of the town and on his way to Penryn. He hadn't been that way since his meeting with John Carter. He smiled ruefully at the way his life had changed since that moment. In common with all folk born and bred in Falmouth, Jan had scant respect for the inhabitants of its smaller rival. It wasn't a malicious rivalry any more, Jan often laughed as he recalled what his father used to say: "The only good thing about Penryn is the road going out" and he would go on to relate the horrific tales of rivalry and bloodshed. It seemed that the rivalry had grown up in conjunction with many other neighbouring towns in Cornwall based on petty jealousy and an inbred fear that one was being outdone by the other. For Jan, the intensity of feeling was little more than a joke, indeed, he had many friends in Penryn, but that did not stop him savouring the sweet smell of success when he rowed in the summer races and managed to pilot his craft to the harbour steps before those of his small town rivals. Compared with the plight of the miners it didn't bear comparison.

He reached the first row of cottages that fronted the Penryn river and decided it was time to go back. Suddenly from out of the shadows that surrounded the old dock gates a group of men emerged. Before he realised what was happening they had surrounded him. Two of the men grabbed his arms and held them tightly behind his back.

Jan tried to struggle free but it was impossible.

"'Tis no use struggling, Mr Pendray, them's the strongest pair of hands this side of Botallack."

Jan, confused as he was at such a turn of events, was surprised that they should know his name.

"What do you want of me?" He demanded, still trying to break the vice-like grip on his arms.

His answer was an extra twist that sent him spinning along the road into Penryn. There was no escape so Jan was forced to go along with the demands of his captors. They trudged on quietly, Jan's efforts to engage in conversation being met by a wall of silence.

On the outskirts of the town the six men who had acted as escorts, were met by another two who held the reins of nine horses. Jan could see by their size that they were the sturdy, little nags that roamed the open moorland to the west. They were game enough and took their riders with no complaint. Jan was puzzled, apart from the soreness of his arms, the men had shown no ill respect towards him. His wrists were tied to the reins but they made sure he was comfortable in the saddle. His escorts still refused to engage in conversation.

Jan had no choice but to resign himself to following his captors' wishes. He settled down in the saddle and let the sturdy nag convey him up the hill to, he knew not where. After two hours Jan had no idea where he was, they had branched off the main route soon after leaving Penryn and were now somewhere in the granite mass that formed the backbone of central Cornwall. The landscape looked the same in the dark and any thoughts of escape quickly faded from Jan's mind. After what seemed a lifetime, the group came to a halt and the man who appeared to be the leader, manoeuvred his pony back until he was at Jan's shoulder.

"Sorry to put 'ee to this trouble, Mr Pendray but 'tis a matter of great importance that you come with us. If you promise not to escape I'll untie your hands, 'tis a mite treacherous, this last bit."

"It seems I have no option, sir, as I have no idea where I am."

The man untied his hands and led him down a narrow path that only allowed single file. Jan had developed a sneaking admiration for the little pony who had guided him so surely for the last two hours. He took care to see that precipitous descent was not too much of a burden for the sweating animal, holding back the reins when a shower of shale slipped past and talking confidently in its ear. After another hour of precarious riding Jan could see the dim lights of a town. There was no doubting it now, they were in mining territory. Huge stacks rose majestically into the night sky still belching forth the smoke that kept the pumps working thousands of feet below. Jan was again gripped by the peculiar feeling he had experienced in Redruth. This was a world apart from his way of life and he began to feel trepidation for what the group of men had in store for him.

All was quiet in the town, the glow from partially drawn curtains and the occasional fire burning in a grate gave the only sign that life existed. The men who Jan had already surmised were miners, left the horses outside a small Kiddlewink and led him off on foot. Jan would have dearly liked to have gone inside as the damp, misty rain had penetrated his coat and was dripping uncomfortably down the inside of his breeches. However, he was no given the chance to linger.

The miners stopped outside an undistinguished looking house built of granite and sandstone. The one distinguishing feature was the brass door- knocker that rested imperiously on the door. The leader knocked twice and immediately, it opened.

"You're late," a voice sounded from within.

Jan recognised it immediately. It was Captain Jonas Treventon. He was sitting behind a small table his legs barely able to fit underneath. Jan stepped inside the tiny room relieved to see a friendly face.

"Jan," he boomed. "Nice of 'ee to come."

"I had little option," Jan replied caustically.

The captain threw back his head and roared with laughter. "I hope the boys weren't too hard on 'ee, they do get carried away sometimes when the blood is charged."

The others joined in the laughter and Jan, despite being irritated by the whole episode, could not help joining in.

"I suppose I can't complain, my arms were pinned back, my wrists were tied and my buttocks feel as though they have been through a mincer. Apart from that my treatment was exceptional."

The laughing continued but it was not malicious and Jan felt they were laughing with him rather that at him. Captain Treventon eventually called the group to order.

"Men," he announced, "let me formally introduce you to Jan Pendray, doer of great deeds and the scourge of Excise men and racketeers alike."

Jan acknowledged his introduction, acutely aware that the assembled group were staring at him with interest rather than respect.

"I think you exaggerate, Captain Treventon," he said, "I am no more than a pawn in the dramatic circumstances that have overtaken my life. I have no skills and very little money. I cannot see any reason why you should force me to cross the moor to a mining area where I am a stranger."

"You underestimate yourself, Jan," replied the Mine Captain. "You are famous and a person with which every common soul can identify."

Jan shuffled uncomfortably, unused to being the centre of attention.

Jonas Treventon got up and addressed the rest of the group. "Now men, you have work to do. I will see you all later."

That was the cue for Jan's escort to leave. They slapped him on the back and wished him good luck before returning to the cold rain that was beating against the window outside. Jan was left alone with the Mine Captain.

"Brandy?" Jonas proffered Jan a glass. "Legal import brandy."

He winked at Jan and raised his glass.

Jan took the drink and let the sharp tang sink down to the pit of his stomach. He could hold off his curiosity no longer.

"What is it you want from me?"

The Captain rested his enormous weight on the edge of the table and began.

"When we last met, you said that the conditions in which miners had to live and work was a scandal, well, I'm trying to do something about it, with the help of 50,000 miners, of course. They do work long hours for little reward, 'tis true, but that's not the trouble. There's not enough food to go round, the mine owners are only interested in the amount of work they can squeeze out of their workers for the least price and don't want to be involved in welfare. It's not their fault the miners are starving. The blame lies with those in power up Lunnon and the Corn Merchants who would rather store their corn for export than sell it to the miner and his family. I tell you, Jan, if we have another winter like we had last year there's going to be whole families dying from starvation."

A tear appeared in the corner of the big man's eyes and Jan was left in no doubt as to the intensity of his feelings. Where did he fit in to all this?

"But what can I do to help?" Jan replied desperately.

"Tonight, in the Wesleyan Chapel at Pool there is a meeting. It will be at ten o'clock so we can catch the men before they go on to the night shift. We want you to address that meeting."

Jan sat down with a thud and felt the blood draining from his cheeks.

"Me?" He gasped. "Why me? I don't know anything about the miners."

"That doesn't matter. They all know about you and regard you and John Carter as friends of the working man. They think you will stand up to the merchants and landowners who they hold responsible for their sorry state."

"But I know nothing about mining, one visit down a mine that's all and, what's more, I know a lot of corn merchants who run fair and honest businesses. I agree some have been guilty of hoarding and I do find that hard to take when families are starving, but I am a part of the sea, what do I know?"

"The Cornish miner is little different to the Cornish fisherman, they know about starvation. They too, are slow to stir and cautious of change but they know when things are not right. It needs somebody to stir things up before it is too late. Those in power have got to listen."

Jan shook his head and sighed. "Did Sir James have anything to do with this?"

"Whatever made 'ee think that, Jan?" He replied with mock indignation but was unable to suppress a grin.

"Because he's a wily old devil, I knew that visit to the Ship and Castle wasn't a coincidence."

"It's not his doing that you think the way you do. It was your reaction to conditions underground and how you feel towards the miner, not his. And don't kid yourself, your attitude towards the miners is genuine. 'Tis not often a sea-faring man will go underground, it did not go unnoticed by those who saw you."

Jan sat with his head resting on his hands, he was just beginning to realise the enormity of the situation in which he found himself. There was no doubting the gravity of the miners' plight. If nothing were done the spectre of mass starvation would become a reality. For him to get involved would be a huge commitment, far beyond anything he had ever done before. He was being asked to sit on top of a tinder-box, one spark and the whole mining community of Camborne and Redruth could explode into an uncontrollable wave of violence.

Had he been a cautious man, he would have left the house there and then, but impulsiveness had been part of his nature from the moment he was able to walk.

He raised his head and said, "I'll address your meeting Captain Treventon but I am not promising any more."

The Captain seized Jan's hand. "Good lad. You'll not regret it, I promise."

It was 8.30 and as the meeting was scheduled for 10 o'clock, they sat and chatted until Captain Treventon decided it was time to go.

The rain had eased a little, no longer swirling around the napthene lamps that stood on the corners of the street. They walked briskly past the rows of miners' cottages before stopping outside one that appeared exactly the same as the one's either side. Captain Treventon banged his fist on the door and awaited a reply. A few moments later it was opened by a grey haired woman who, on recognising the Mine captain, beckoned them inside.

"Hello, Beth," he said respectfully, "this is Jan Pendray."

"Come in Captain, like a glass of milk would 'ee?"

Jonas Treventon nodded respectfully and they were ushered into the front room. It was sparsely furnished and cold, the fireplace an empty shell as if waiting for a delivery of wood that had never arrived. The walls were whitewashed and the old curtains that covered the window were frayed at the edges underlying the extent to which the average mining family had sunk. However, despite the lack of luxuries, everything was spotless and nothing could detract from the warmth that the visitor felt when he was invited into the home of a miner.

Jan accepted the glass of milk from the old lady when she returned aware that he was consuming a drink that the house could barely afford.

"How many live here?" He asked politely.

"Just meself and me two daughters, sir. Jack, me old man was killed last year. He got trapped between one of the trucks and the wall, two thousand feet underground. They say he had no chance as it was full and going fast."

She brushed a tear away with the corner of her apron.

The Mine Captain hurriedly downed his glass and, with a word of comfort for the widow, ushered Jan towards the door. Once outside they breathed a sigh of relief. Despite the warmth of their welcome, there was sorrow in the house that hung heavily on anyone who entered.

"How old do you think she is, Jan?"

"About forty, I would say."

"Twenty-seven."

Jan gasped. "I don't believe it."

"'Tis the truth. That's what poverty does for you."

"But surely, the mine pays compensation?"

"Only the first two months after that they don't care. They've satisfied their consciences by paying for the funeral and providing a small amount of subsistence.

From then on people like Beth have to rely on others to see that their children do not starve."

Jan walked on in stony silence, mulling over what the Mine Captain had said. The Captain was clever. He had shown Jan just one example of the poverty that was prevalent in a thousand homes in the same area. The catastrophic effect it was having on a once attractive woman was an image that Jan could not erase from his mind. The premature grey hair, the sunken eyes and the hollow cheeks gave indications of former beauty that had been worn away by the insidious march of hunger.

The main street through Pool joined the two mining communities of Camborne and Redruth so there was still a fair amount of traffic on the road despite the lateness of the hour. Jan was feeling nervous, he had never addressed a meeting before and had little idea of what to expect. Jonas Treventon sensed his tension. "Nothing to worry about Jan, just a few words, that's all."

The presence of the big miner was comforting but did little to quell the rising panic Jan was feeling in the pit of his stomach. This was not helped by the scene they encountered outside the Wesleyan chapel. Captain Treventon had seriously under-estimated the number of miners that would attend the meeting. Jan turned white. As far as he could see, a huge mass of jostling miners were attempting to clamber up the steps and push their way into the hall. Jonas Treventon elbowed his way through, keeping a huge forearm around his protégé until he finally made the relative safety of the chapel ante-room. The line of men who were desperately trying to control the crowd, were fighting a losing battle.

"There's too many inside already, Cap'n," shouted one of the stewards. "What shall we do?"

Jonas took an instant decision. "Bring the lectern outside we'll talk to 'em in the street."

Hurriedly a couple of miners fought their way through to the relative calm of the hall, grabbed the lectern and manhandled it outside. Never before had the instrument of God been away from its omnphallic position at the centre of the congregation but, neither had it been placed in front of such a large gathering.

The Captain turned to Jan. "Few more than I expected but it's a compliment to you and an indication of how desperate things are."

Jan's mouth was dry. In the semi-darkness outside he could see hundreds of glowing lamps and a sea of faces that went on way beyond his level of vision. He was seized with an overwhelming desire to run, to escape from this madhouse and be sitting by the fire in the Ship and Castle so that he could shut himself away from the realities of a situation over which he had no control. He wanted to encircle himself in a cocoon of selfishness and pretend that this was not happening. But there was no escape. He dimly heard the booming voice of the Mine Captain as he called for silence from the crowd. Gradually the noise died down. They wanted to hear what the speakers had to offer.

"Friends and fellow miners," the Captain bellowed, " 'tis an indication to you all, this is no revivalist meeting but a meeting to show the men who run this county of ours, how we feel about our women and children starving to death."

Roars of approval rang out from the assembled masses.

"And to prove we are not alone in our cause, we have with us, not a miner but a true friend who seeks justice for our cause. I give you Jan Pendray."

There was a short pause and then a crescendo of cheering as Jan was squeezed up to the lectern. The bewildered Jan stood for a full minute waiting for the applause to stop. He was beginning to realise that his feats of courage and daring were becoming known to a wider audience. The knowledge that he lent support to a living legend had spread through the mining fraternity, they saw Jan as someone who could make people in authority, listen. Swimming across Mounts Bay to avoid the Excisemen only served to embellish his burgeoning reputation.

Taking a deep breath and grabbing the lectern to stop his hands shaking, he started to speak.

"Friends, I am not a miner but a man of the sea. I have been down a mine only once but the sea is in my veins the same way as copper and tin is in yours- we are made of the same cloth. Often the sea will take life and often the mine will become a grave, 'tis what we expect. But never," he paused. "Never my friends, has the sea or mine been allowed to dictate the pattern of our existence. It gives us satisfaction to defy the elements God has placed on this earth. We may burrow deep or sail far and return knowing we have done a fair day's work. No man worth his salt is afraid of work. It is the lifeblood of existence and the way to a man's respect and self-esteem. But what of that man if he comes home weary and finds that there is no food to feed himself and his family?"

Jan had no idea where the words came from but he shouted the last sentence with such vehemence that the crowd roared in agreement. From somewhere inside him he had touched the very nerve that ran through the beleaguered mining community.

"We are not asking for money," he continued, "although we could do with it. All we want is to be able to feed and clothe our families so they can survive the winter. Is that not too much to ask?"

A roar of approval went up from those able to hear. It was quickly passed on to those at the back until the voices of ten thousand miners filled the night sky. Jan was one of them now, his eyes glinted and passion oozed from every pore.

"And who's to blame for this? Not the miners, not the fishermen, not the working classes. It's the law makers sitting in their plush offices, the gentry who do little else than live off the fat of the land and, above all, the Corn Merchants who refuse to sell their stock, preferring to export to wealthier markets abroad. They're the ones who keep the miners starving."

The intensity with which Jan delivered his words drew the audience to fever pitch. One word from him and the meeting could spiral out of control. A cold sweat broke out on his forehead as he realised what he had done. He had turned a placid, good-humoured crowd into a baying mass of hatred, hell bent on exacting revenge on the Corn Merchants who they now held responsible for their desperate plight.

Captain Treventon too, had noticed the change of mood. He stepped in front of Jan and, holding his arms up, addressed the throng.

"The time will come my friends," he called out, "but not yet. Those in authority will not ignore this meeting tonight. Go, tell your friends that tonight, we have started a crusade that will mean a better deal for everyone."

With the cheers ringing in his ears, he led Jan away from the lectern and back into the relative quiet of the chapel. Once inside he sensed Jan's mood. "It was getting dangerous, Jan, you've a manner about you that fires the bellies of normal men. One more spark and we would have a riot on our hands. As it is, there are bound to be questions asked."

"Wasn't that what you wanted?" Jan replied irritably. He rather enjoyed it once he got going.

"Nay, Jan, 'tis not the right moment. You're a mite quick-tempered for your own good. There'll be a next time, don't' 'ee fret."

He put a massive arm around him and smiled. Jan heaved a sigh and began to realise that his impulsiveness nearly got the better of him once again.

"You're right Captain Treventon," he agreed. "I never realised the power of the spoken word. They actually listened to me and I am not a miner. Do they usually display that kind of passion?"

"Only when it is a matter of life and death. Show me any man who would not fight for the right of his family to have food on their table and clothes to keep out the dank of winter?"

Jan scratched his chin. "You are sure it is the lack of food that angers them and not the conditions in which they have to work?"

"A miner will work in any conditions, just as long as he can earn enough to keep the wolf from the door. 'Tis not often you see a miner leave the ground, it is in their blood. Sometimes a mine owner will take advantage but often they are little better off than the miners themselves. The vast majority around here are decent, God-fearing men who have come along tonight hoping desperately that we can do something for them."

Sitting alone in the back pew of the chapel, the two men felt the weight of responsibility on their shoulders. Singing had started outside so after a moment's contemplation they went out to join the throng. The new Methodist hymns blended in well with the traditional mining songs as the sound rose sweetly into the dark Cornish sky. Eventually the crowd dwindled and the austere granite chapel between the two mining towns resort resumed its customary respectful silence.

CHAPTER 14

It was a couple of days later that a small column about the meeting appeared in the Falmouth Packet. Meg threw the paper at him as he lay in bed. She had not really forgiven him for disappearing without as much as a note of explanation. Any amount of protest from Jan about him not having a choice, had fallen on deaf ears. Jan put it down to the contrariness of women and laughed it off, although he may have thought differently if he had seen the mask of worry that had clouded her face when he had failed to return that night.

It was not much of a report although it did make the front page. It read as follows:

On Tuesday evening, at the Pool Wesleyan Chapel, a meeting was held by the miners of that parish. Addressing the meeting was Jan Pendray, known associate and friend of the notorious smuggler John Carter, who is, at present, serving a 12 month jail sentence for burglary. The purpose of the meeting was to air the grievances of the miners who feel they are being unjustly treated by the authorities in not providing enough food for their families. Some reports suggest that there were 5000 present at the gathering which, at one time, spilled onto the road that links Camborne and Redruth.

Mr Pendray accompanied by Mine Captain, Jonas Treventon of Wheal Cupid, spoke of the sorry plight the miners were in at present, with little food to face the winter. They blame it on the Corn Merchants who refuse to sell their grain at a price they could afford.

The meeting was brought to an end by the singing of hymns and psalms.

Jan read it a dozen times. He could not fault the accuracy although he would have liked it to be longer. A gathering of 5000 people was not a trifling event.

"Perhaps, now," he thought, "the people who run this county of ours will take notice."

He placed the broadsheet on the bedside table and swung his legs to the ground, there were barrels to shift.

As it turned out, the meeting had little noticeable effect and by Christmas, the lot of the miner was a good deal worse. Horrific rumours were rife, children dying in their cots, dogs being slaughtered for meat, respectable ladies offering their services for a price of a meal and in one case, a miner who had eaten the flesh of his own son who had died the previous evening.

Jan could not help feeling responsible and consequently, he was difficult to live with, the sheer frustration of being unable to help preyed on his mind to such an extent that he was incapable of holding a civil conversation with anyone. Meg was not pleased. She could handle him but was unable to tolerate his rudeness to the customers. She knew her livelihood depended on a smile of welcome.

One morning in late January, Jan was still in bed. Meg had developed the habit of getting up early and bringing him breakfast at ten o'clock. However, on this occasion she came empty-handed.

"There's a person downstairs wanting to see you," she stated coolly. "Shall I send him up?"

Jan groaned from beneath the bedspread. "Who wants to see me at this hour?"

"It is ten o'clock Jan, if you haven't noticed," she replied curtly.

"Who is it?"

"He wouldn't say, he's waiting downstairs……"

She was cut short by a voice from behind.

"Jan, you lazy landlubber, what kind of welcome is this for a friend?"

Jan shot up on recognising the voice. "John, when did you get out?"

John Carter laughed. "Let me go last night, got remission for good conduct. I'm on my way back to Prussia Cove."

Jan scrambled out of bed and the two men embraced each other, delight showing on both their faces.

Despite his jovial manner, Jan was quick to see what eight months at His Majesty's pleasure had done for John Carter. He was thinner and the skin across his cheeks was drawn and sallow. His eyes still contained the old sparkle but they had sunk deep into his face casting dark shadows across his forehead.

John sensed his reaction. "Aye, I know I'm not the person I was, but nothing a couple of weeks of sea air and Bessie's cooking won't put right."

Jan stood looking at his friend not realising how much he had missed him. "You must stay and have something to eat. I'm sure Bessie won't mind waiting a little longer."

"Well damn me for a thing, Jan, inviting me for breakfast and not even a word of introduction to this fine young woman who kindly let me in."

Meg blushed and noted Jan's embarrassment.

"Meg, this is John Carter, otherwise known as the King of Prussia."

John Carter took Meg's hand and kissed it with relish. "'Tis a pleasure to make the acquaintance of such a beautiful lady."

Meg smiled. "The pleasure is mine, sir. It's nice to be paid a compliment once in a while. I'll get breakfast for you right away."

With that she left the room.

"Fine girl, Jan," mused John looking appreciatively at Meg's well-shaped form as it drifted out of the door.

"Yes," replied Jan uncomfortably. "She has been good to me in more ways than one, I fear that I may not have shown my gratitude as much as I might. The truth is, I have had a lot on my mind of late."

"I heard in Truro that you have been setting yourself up as champion of the miners."

"A spokesman, that's all, nothing has come of it."

"Are the miners that badly off?"

Jan's face clouded. "You have no idea the appalling conditions in which they are supposed to live and work. It's iniquitous that such conditions should be allowed to prevail. If times are hard, you and I can live off the sea. Those poor souls have nothing but the food they can find in the markets. Most of them haven't got any land on which to rear a few chickens or plant potatoes."

John could see the intensity burning in his eyes. At times like that he was too emotional for his own good.

"I know how the miners feel, Jan, I've suffered for the last eight months for the sake of so called justice. Not that I object, I committed a crime which deserved punishment. But the conditions in which I was held defy belief. I shared a cell with fourteen others who will have to endure the smell, disease and inedible food for a lot longer than I. It was a never ending battle to stop yourself from being eaten alive by the rats that infest every part of the prison block. It's a crime that the do-gooders of the ruling classes turn a blind eye to, the indignity and degradation to which they condemn their fellow man."

Jan was shocked. Prison had changed his friend, before he had never showed a trace of resentment or bitterness. Life wasn't a game any more. Both of them had been forced to look out from their own cosy world and accept that life outside Prussia Cove was not a bed of roses.

Once Jan had dressed, they went downstairs to be greeted by the gratifying smell of bacon and eggs coming from the kitchen.

John drank in the smell with relish. "You've carved out a cosy existence here, Jan. What of Anna?"

Jan smiled. "I saw her before Christmas. She is betrothed to our mutual friend Peter Pendennis."

John whistled. "I bet that went down well with you."

Jan hesitated before saying, "I would be a liar if I said I did not think of her and I have to admit she is still able to rule my heart above my head at times. As time goes on the feelings get weaker. When I see her, the old attraction is still there but I have Meg now. She doesn't rule my heart in the same way but I feel great affection for her."

John sighed. "You're a hard man Jan Pendray. You don't know when you are well off. That girl worships the ground you walk on. I can see it in her face, she will do anything for you but don't push her too far or you'll lose her."

At that point Meg came in carrying two plates laden with fried bacon rashers and new laid eggs delivered that morning from her sister's farm in Constantine.

"'Tis a good cook you are to go with your good looks, Meg," laughed John as he tucked into the first fresh food he had tasted in eight months.

Meg acknowledged the compliment and watched them eat. It was the first time she had seen Jan smile in days.

John Carter stayed well into the afternoon, chatting about his experiences and letting Jan show him around the Falmouth waterfront where he had spent so much of his youth. He eventually left with a promise to keep in touch and a pledge to let Jan know if anything came up. Of that they needed to say no more.

That night Jan persuaded Meg to close early and they retired to the lounge with a bottle of Burgundy that he had unearthed from the depths of the cellar. They sat arm in arm watching the logs spit and crackle sending a shower of sparks up the granite chimney.

"I'm sorry, Meg," Jan whispered softly. "I know I've neglected you recently and I've let my frustration show on the customers."

Meg put her finger to his lips. "Don't say any more. I understand."

Jan was unable to stop a tear fall unashamedly onto her hand. The intensity of the moment had loosened the mask that he had inscrutably held since the day his father had died. It didn't matter, Meg was crying too, her tears born out of the love she felt for a man who could turn her world to sweetness and light with a few simple words.

In the ensuing weeks Jan delivered a number of impassioned speeches to the miners of Camborne and Redruth and, in so doing, developed a reputation as a stirring orator. It did him good as he felt he was doing something worthwhile but it appeared to be doing precious little for the miner. The food shortage that had given most families a miserable Christmas got much worse.

Of John Carter, he heard very little, only that he was back at Prussia Cove. There had been no news of any cargoes reaching the coast. On a Thursday, in late February, the silence was broken. A note was delivered to the Ship and Castle. It read:

Jan and Meg,
Have secured two tickets for the Penzance Mariners and Shipwright's Ball on Saturday 25th March. Won't take no for an answer- see you at Bessies on Friday,
John.

Jan showed the note to Meg and grinned. Her face was ashen.

"I couldn't, Jan," she protested. "All those people. 'Tis the social event of the year in Penzance, I would feel out of place in such grand company."

Jan put an arm on both shoulders and looked her straight in the eye. "With your beauty and that radiant smile you will melt a thousand hearts."

Meg was not to be soft-soaped, a surge of panic had started to rise from the pit of her stomach and she had no armoury to deal with it. She had never mixed in such exalted circles and the thought of it sent her into paroxysms of terror.

"And I have nothing to wear," she added limply.

"That's easily solved. We will go to Mitchells and hire the finest outfit we can afford."

Meg was not convinced. "All the aristocracy and well-to-does in Cornwall would be there, we should look like fools. Those gatherings are not for the likes of us."

Jan sighed. "If you feel that, I'll send a reply to John saying we cannot make it."

Meg's repost was a little too hasty. "I've never been to a ball before. Do you think they would announce our names? And have proper waiters with silver salvers? And real musicians? And ladies with fans?"

Jan laughed. "So you'll come then?"

Meg gripped his arm. "You must promise me that you will not leave my side for one second. I would die of embarrassment if I had to speak to anyone."

"Good, that's settled then," replied Jan and went off to open the bar.

For the next couple of days Meg was like a schoolgirl. She tried on her entire wardrobe in a variety of combinations, all of which had to be approved by a hapless Jan. At first, he watched with amused toleration but, having exhausted all the possible combinations, Jan put his foot down and sent her off to Mitchell's, the finest clothes store in Falmouth. Suspecting another bout of scrutinising, Jan refused to go with her, finding the idea of fishing off the pier an infinitely more satisfying occupation.

When she returned, Jan was not allowed the merest glimpse at what was in the boxes that filled the floor of the snug. He amused himself by trying to discover the contents but was given short shrift, secretly enjoying the enthusiasm Meg showed for her impending entry into the upper echelons of Cornish society. After the way he had behaved over the last few weeks, he was glad to be able to redress the balance.

They left for Prussia Cove on Friday afternoon. It was the first time Meg had left the Inn but she was confident that Jamie Fidock, a retired mariner who had run an Inn before, would ensure that nothing untoward would happen while they were away. It was cold but mercifully the rain had eased and, although the route was muddy, they made good progress for the time of year. Meg kept glancing over her shoulder to check that the boxes were still securely fastened to the saddle. They reached Bessies at 6 o'clock. Although it was getting dark, the sharp outline of the sea was clearly visible as it merged with the dark clouds on the horizon. They could hear the waves gently lapping on the sand below.

Bessie, on hearing the horses, was outside the door ready to welcome her guests.

"Come on in, me dears, 'tis good to see you again, Jan, my handsome, how have 'ee been keeping?"

"Well, thanks, Bessie," Jan replied helping Meg off her horse. He introduced her to Bessie with an exaggerated flourish.

They hurried into the warmth of the lounge and spread their hands in front of the glowing fire.

"My, John was right, you are a fine looking girl and that's for sure."

Meg blushed and said nothing, overawed by the enormity of the hulk of a woman that filled the tiny room.

"John'll be here shortly, make yourselves comfy and I'll bring you some hot soup."

They drew two chairs close to the range and let the warmth filter through their damp clothing.

Meg turned to Jan in wonder. "Jan, she's huge, why didn't you tell me?"

Jan grinned. "Never mention a woman's weight."

Meg slapped his arm and pretended not to feel the soreness caused by two hours in the saddle.

John Carter eventually arrived apologising profusely for not being there to welcome them to Prussia Cove. They spent the rest of the evening in pleasant conversation and Meg's fear of Bessie evaporated once she realised that there was not an ounce of malice in the large woman's nature. They did, however, discover that John was to take Bessie as his partner to the Ball.

The next morning John insisted on showing Meg the delights of Prussia Cove. Jan, meanwhile, was able to persuade one of the local fishermen to let him accompany him on his daily boat trip to pull lobster pots in Mounts Bay. After a late lunch, Meg retired, leaving the two men to talk.

"Well, what's been happening, John?" Enquired Jan anxious not to miss out on anything.

John lowered his voice. "I've made a couple of runs over to France myself in the last few days, things are not the same. There is all kinds of trouble brewing over there, Madame le Guillotine is doing a roaring trade by all accounts, so it's little wonder that the French are cautious. But it's more than that. In three separate areas of Brittany the contacts I trusted with my life, did not want to know. Why do you think that is?"

Jan scratched his chin and thought for a moment. "I can only think of two reasons; one, they have stopped illicit trading for something more profitable or, two, someone else has moved in whilst you were away."

"Exactly! Convenient wasn't it? So I made some enquiries. Apparently boats are still carrying liquor from France and, on a much larger scale, four hundred tonners which can only be docked in Falmouth. As you know, the Excise Authority there is the strictest in Cornwall, with each boat being searched thoroughly before they are allowed to unload. So how do they do it?"

Jan was mystified.

"I'll tell you how they do it. By dropping anchor off Pendennis Head, throwing the contraband overboard in water-tight containers and bringing them into Swanpool under cover of darkness."

"Ingenious and effective," murmured Jan. "Swanpool has a sand beach which runs up to the road, it would be easy to drive mules to the water's edge, load 'em up and away within twenty minutes."

"What worries me is that this is smuggling on a far greater scale than before. In the past we have been able to get away with it purely by being regarded as a harmless trade which appealed to those of a romantic nature. Those in authority were prepared to turn a blind eye providing there was the occasional reward. Now it is bound to attract attention from more important quarters."

"Do you think Pendennis has anything to do with this?"

"I've no proof yet, but I'll put a guinea to a farthing that he is mixed up with it along the line. It all adds up, me out of the way, boats coming into Falmouth and him living close by."

"He's playing a dangerous game if he is?"

"Aye, but think of the profit he can make on just one run, we could never bring in the same amount with our boats, they are all too small."

Although ignorant of the economics of smuggling, it did not take Jan too much thought to work out that Peter Pendennis could make a fortune. Jan mulled it over and kept coming back to the same conclusion.

"The question is, what can we do about it?" Jan asked eventually.

"Very little, we have no proof."

"What could be done if you had proof?"

John Carter considered carefully. "Again,very little. I suppose we could inform the Militia but it would go against all the principles by which I live. I may not like my livelihood being taken away but I don't feel inclined to stoop to such base lengths to get it back. Smuggling has always been an honourable business."

"But Pendennis nearly had you hanged," cried Jan vehemently. "Surely that ranks higher than any smugglers charter?"

"We don't know for sure."

"We do, at least, I do. When I met him in Falmouth before Christmas he denied any knowledge of Sergeant Crowlas. I knew that wasn't true because I saw them together in Bodmin the day before the trial. I could tell they weren't talking about the weather, what more proof do you need?"

John Carter did not reply. He had known all along that Pendennis was the cause of his demise but he wasn't prepared to admit it to anyone. Some people had short memories. Not John Carter, he would announce it to the world when he was good and ready.

It was getting late so the two men finished their discussion and went off to prepare for the evening's entertainment. Jan found the door to his roomed locked and no amount of pleading would get Meg to open it. His clothes for the evening had been placed neatly on a chair and he was forced to use a spare room across the landing. In half an hour he had washed, shaved and put on the only suit he had, it was his father's. Fortunately his broad shoulders squeezed into the jacket and, although he felt like a trussed chicken, a glance in the mirror confirmed he was satisfied with his appearance. With a wry grin at the locked door he went downstairs.

He stood with his back to the fire and was unable to control a tingle of anticipation as he heard Meg's footsteps on the stairs. Despite that he was totally unprepared for what he saw. She was stunning. Her black hair was tied in bunches that cascaded prettily over her bare shoulders. The dress she wore was made of shining blue satin gathered in at the waist and cut as low as modesty would allow giving ample prominence to her well- rounded breasts. Draped loosely over her shoulders was a white lace shawl with fine stitching that, if she but knew it, was all the rage in Parisian society. She stood there uncertainly, her demure shyness adding to the radiance of her beauty.

Jan let out a low whistle, he had been prepared to make the conventional platitudes on her appearance but the sight of her had taken his breath away.

"You look simply gorgeous," he breathed.

"Do you like it?" she said nervously fingering the satin dress.

"Come here," he said holding out his arms. "The dress is matched only by the magnificence of the person inside it. Meg, I will be so proud to have you on my arm."

He leant forward and kissed her gently on the cheek.

"Well me dear 'tis nice you look and no mistake," Bessie said as she swept into the room behind them. She, too, was wearing a long dress but as it was not gathered in at the waist, it hid the roundness of her figure. Jan realised for the first time, that if she were a few stone lighter, she would be a very attractive woman."

John, who had been outside to check that the chaise he had ordered from Marazion had arrived, called out that it was time to go, so, in eager anticipation, the party set forth for Penzance.

The road was crowded with all manner of horse-drawn vehicles each conveying their occupants to the highlight of the social calendar in West Cornwall. They arrived outside the Municipal building shortly after eight o'clock. Jan, despite his outward air of confidence, was as nervous as Meg. He had never been to such an illustrious gathering and he was thankful for the presence of John and Bessie who seemed to be at ease in such grand company.

Once inside, the ladies and gentlemen were relieved of their cloaks by an exemplary looking steward in a blazing red coat and starched white cuffs who whisked them away with the minimum of fuss. They joined a small queue of people who were waiting to be announced.

"This should be interesting," whispered John as he handed the invitation cards to the announcer stood by the ballroom door. They stood waiting their turn as the announcer called out the names of the people in front, to the complete indifference of the gathered assembly within. Meg and Jan were called first.

"Mrs.M Tremaine and Mr. J Pendray."

The gentle buzz of conversation ebbed for a moment as the guests scrutinised the couple.

"Miss B Benyon and ..." the announcer gave a small cough. "And Mr J Carter alias, the King of Prussia."

All conversation in the room ceased and everyone turned towards the upright figure of John Carter. John had added the title King of Prussia himself and was a little surprised the announcer had read it out.

They stood there in complete silence. "Perhaps there are a few consciences being pricked by our arrival," murmured John and out loud to Jan he stated. "It will be a pleasure to eat good food instead of bread and water, Jan."

The incident passed off with a buzz of veiled whispering. Meg was petrified.

"Everyone is looking at us, Jan," she hissed clenching his arm with all her might.

"It does appear we have caused a bit of a stir," he replied calmly, obviously enjoying the moment.

The tension was broken by the arrival of Sir James Aubyne at Jan's shoulder.

"A pleasure to see you again, Jan." he said grasping his hand.

"The pleasure is mutual," he replied sincerely. "I have been wanting to see you for some time. It was you who set me up all along, wasn't it?"

A twinkle appeared in St. Aubyne's eye. "Set up is hardly fair, I merely set the facts out before your eyes, your conscience and eloquence did the rest."

Jan grinned and sipped from a glass of champagne that had been placed in his hand, wryly noting that Meg's glass was already empty.

"I fear though, my impassioned pleas have done little to further the cause of the miners. It appears the influential souls here tonight are only interested in lining their already swollen wallets rather than channel some of their wealth towards helping those who are starving."

Jan felt his anger rise.

"No, Jan, not all here tonight are unsympathetic. Unfortunately, unless the Government are made aware of the gravity of the situation, very little can be done. We need far more food than it is possible to grow in Cornwall."

"How do you propose to make the Government aware?"

The Lord looked troubled. "I had stored some faith in my prestige as a landowner. I wrote letters to the Prime Minister but the response has been nothing more than a polite acknowledgement. We need action rather than words if we are to prevent a human catastrophe. If nothing is done quickly I fear we will have a full scale riot on our hands."

Jan shrugged. "It may not be a bad thing if it is the only way to get people to take notice."

Lord St. Aubyne shook his head.

"A riot would cause bloodshed. I could not countenance such an extreme measure."

Jan let the matter rest and turned to the adjoining room where the violins were being screeched into tune in preparation for the first dance.

"Shall we go next door, Meg?" He enquired. His mistress readily agreed and, with a polite bow to Lord St. Aubyne, he led her to the music that had now changed from the awful cacophony to the pleasant strains of a Viennese Waltz.

Jan was not cut out to be a dancer so he was relieved when all the guests had been announced and he heard the call for the buffet to be served. The double doors on the opposite side of the hall were flung open to reveal table upon table of exquisitely presented food. It was a gargantuan sight, with each table sporting a theme- fish from Newlyn, meats from the local farms and specialities from the East India Spice Company. Unlike a lot of functions at the time where guests were seated and waited upon by a convoy of waiters, the food was laid out in such a way that those present could help themselves. As befitted a fishing port, there was soused mackerel, fresh lobsters and star-gazy pie interspersed by a selection of oriental fruits shipped in from the West Indies especially for the occasion.

Meg stared at the feast in wonder.

"I've never seen so much food," she gasped.

Jan found it nauseating and could not contain his anger as he watched the rich, pot-bellied men gorge themselves with obvious relish. However, not wishing to disappoint Meg, he took a modest amount on his plate and sat quietly in the corner. He had always enjoyed lobster, getting a special thrill every time he lifted his father's pots, but that was before he had seen the effects of starvation first hand.

Meg, having overcome her initial nerves, was enjoying herself immensely. The champagne had given her confidence and she was able to enjoy the countless compliments that were paid to her during the course of the evening. Such was her popularity that Jan was able to leave her as she was whisked off to take part in the gavottes and minuets in the hall next door.

Jan did not see much of John although he often caught glimpses of Bessie through the milling throng. Whilst Meg was dancing, he wandered out of the dining area and made for the smoking room. Although he hated smoking he was prepared to tolerate the muggy atmosphere for the sake of a quiet drink away from the noise and bustle.

A group of men were lounging in easy chairs, all were elderly and seeking refuge from the noise of music and prattling wives. Jan sat himself down in a vacant chair and poured himself a drink from the cut glass decanter that was placed on the table in the middle of the room. One man offered him snuff but he declined politely.

"Damned if I can stand that rumpus," one of the elderly gentlemen declared. "Bit of peace and quiet is what I need."

"Too old for that kind of carry on," replied another. "'Tis alright for those young bucks who spend their day chasing pretty wenches. Wasn't like that in our day- had to work all hours of the day and night to keep the wolf from the door."

Jan listened with faint amusement wondering if he too, would become cynical of all youngsters and their disrespectful behaviour, when he grew old. He noted that he was the youngest in the room by at least thirty years.

"What brings you in here young fellow?" The question was fired at Jan by a man with grey hair and a white moustache that had been exquisitely manicured for the occasion.

Jan coughed. "I find your conversation more agreeable than the ghastly screeching of the violin."

They smiled in agreement.

"And to be honest, I was getting uncomfortable looking at all that food when there are thousands of miners surviving on nothing but barley bread and limpets."

The old men shifted uncomfortably in their chairs.

"'Tis true, the miner does not get much to eat these days," the grey haired man replied. "But we are too old. It is up to people of your age to do something about it."

"That cannot be true," argued Jan. "You are all Cornishmen and, if I am not mistaken, men of considerable influence. It is people like you the miner needs, those in authority will listen to what you have to say."

The old men stirred nervously. They agreed with his sentiment but hid behind their age, using it as an excuse to absolve them of any responsibility towards their fellow Cornishmen.

Jan pressed on. "I don't accept age as an excuse to do nothing. You could always do something, however small."

The man with the grey hair stared at Jan, his face giving nothing away.

"You have a persuasive tongue young man, what is your name?"

"Jan Pendray, sir."

"I've heard that name before somewhere. I seem to recall a chap called Pendray got into trouble with the Militia in Penzance. Rumour had it, he escaped by swimming across Mounts Bay."

"That was me," Jan replied flatly, he could see no reason to deny it.

"Damn me, 'twas a rare old swim, did you really do it?"

Jan nodded. "Yes, but I wouldn't recommend it as a good thing for yourselves."

They laughed with delight, glad to share their bonhomie with the young gentleman who had honoured them with his presence.

The talk continued to switch from topic to topic with amazing speed and, although Jan enjoyed their witty repartee, it was evident that advancing years had crushed the intensity of thought that had guided their lives in the past. Jan did not mind, he found the conversation amusing and without malice but he could not erase from his mind, the poor half-starved community that was barely a horse- ride away.

Eventually he got up to leave.

The grey haired old gentleman took him by the arm and led him to the door.

"'Don't be too hard on them Mr Pendray," he whispered. " They are farmers who know what a bad harvest can do. They don't understand what it is like to work underground. They've all faced starvation at some point in their lives."

"I can assure you, sir, I have nothing but admiration for them all," he replied sincerely, shaking the man's bony hand with genuine respect. "But it does not stop me trying to influence whoever I can in order that something is done."

"Well, good luck Mr. Pendray, I have a feeling we may hear more of you one day."

With that, he drifted back to the others and left Jan to pursue the delights that were in full swing on the other side of the door.

Once outside he bumped into John Carter.

"Are you enjoying yourself, Jan?"

"I'm beginning to," he admitted. "It takes some getting used to- all this ostentation while miners are starving."

John laughed. "It's no good thinking you can save the world, Jan. There are plenty of good men here. It's not a crime to possess money. Most have worked hard for it. We all feel for the miners but there is only so much we can do. It is up to Government to solve the problem."

Jan felt slightly ashamed, his thinking of the guests had been coloured by his own experiences in Camborne and Redruth. He knew deep down that not all the rich were guilty.

"But there's one that has not done a day's work in his life." Jan had caught a glimpse of Peter Pendennis who was watching a group of men gambling at a table placed beside the dance floor.

"Aye, I've seen him," said John, his voice hardening. "I've a mind to have a chat with him later."

That opportunity came quicker than he anticipated. Pendennis had spotted Jan and sauntered over.

"Well Jan, it is a pleasure to see you again. I hope our last meeting is forgotten." He delivered the greeting with a disarming smile that immediately raised Jan's hackles.

Pendennis turned to John Carter.

"Mr. Carter I believe- I don't think we have met."

He offered John his hand. Caught momentarily off guard he hesitated and then shook it firmly.

"No, we have not had the pleasure," he replied smoothly. "It is an honour to shake the hand of such a distinguished gentleman and businessman. It is so nice to meet people face to face."

The last remark was delivered with just a hint of sarcasm that did not go unnoticed by Jan who was fully prepared for trouble.

Pendennis, however, appeared not to notice and went on, "I hope you are enjoying the party. It is perhaps, a trifle boring but enjoyable, nonetheless."

Conversation had ceased as those nearby sensed the tension.

John Carter, who had struggled to keep his temper, replied cuttingly, "I experience not the slightest boredom. It makes an agreeable change from slimy, dark walls and the smell of rotting humanity."

Pendennis stroked his chin. "I did hear of your unfortunate internment, very sad business, Jan and I were only discussing it before Christmas."

Jan decided to say nothing and join the silent onlookers who were hanging on every word that was exchanged.

"'Tis a pity," John continued, "that those who condemn their fellow men to such degradation, cannot experience for themselves the conditions that prevail in our prisons today."

"I have heard they are bad, especially in Bodmin, in fact, I have just started a trust with a view to improving that very problem. A move that I am sure will meet with your approval."

It was a masterstroke delivered at exactly the right moment. A spontaneous round of applause broke out and neither John nor Jan could think of anything to say.

After a few moments, John regained his poise.

"A laudable gesture no doubt created by conscience."

"We must all accept some of the blame for the unpleasant conditions in our jails. I am in the fortunate position to be able to do something about it."

Another round of applause caused Pendennis to puff out his cheeks and smile benignly at those around him. What they did not know was the interest that Peter Pendennis' father had shown in his new- found wealth and where it was obtained. Setting up a charity meant that he did not have to answer difficult questions. It had also been of immense benefit in his relationship with Anna. She was overwhelmed by his generosity and had given her undivided attention to the scheme.

Jan could stay silent no longer.

"And may we ask where you get the money to finance such a scheme?"

The crowd around the discussion pressed closer.

"You may and I will tell you. Since we last met I have set up my own Corn exporting business which, although still in its infancy, is already building a steady profit. I do not like the vulgarity of wealth so I have chosen to donate the profits to a worthwhile cause."

To John and Jan it sounded too good to be true. Peter Pendennis? Champion of the underprivileged? But it was not a view shared by those others who were witness to the conversation. They shook his hand, slapped his back and smothered him with sycophantic praise. Pendennis beamed and revelled in his popularity.

Jan turned away in disgust. "Come, John let us find the ladies and leave this pillar of the establishment to his own devices."

He took his friend's arm and ushered him away from what was becoming a highly explosive situation. John's face was dark, his grey eyes narrow and cold. Reluctantly he allowed himself to be led away.

Jan had seen the signs. "This isn't the time or place, John. You'll get your chance soon enough."

"I could kill that man in cold blood," he muttered darkly. "Talking like that. I've helped more people in distress than that arrogant prig ever has and he knows it."

His anger subsided as quickly as it had arisen and soon he was chatting amiably on more mundane matters as they searched for the ladies on the crowded dance floor.

Meg was still going strong. She had worn out at least a dozen would-be suitors and after two exhausting gavottes with Jan, he too had to admit defeat and left her to it. Flushed with champagne and wine he staggered up the carpeted stairs to the gentlemen's room. As he was about to enter the door of the ladies' powder room opened and out walked Anna. They stopped and stared at each other in uncomfortable silence.

Jan was the first to recover.

"Anna, you look positively charming."

She blushed and made to go.

"Wait, I must talk to you."

"No, we mustn't, Jan. Peter would not like it."

Before she could move he took her arm and led her forcibly into a room on the other side of the landing which had been set aside for the cloaks and capes of the guests downstairs. A solitary candle burned on the mantelpiece.

"Jan, let me go," Anna pleaded desperately. "If Peter finds us..."

"One minute, Anna. That is all I ask- please."

She hesitated and Jan released his grip.

"Don't marry him. It would be a ghastly mistake which you would regret for the rest of your life. All he cares about is himself."

"That is not true," she cried, leaping to the defence of her betrothed. "Why, only last week he set up a fund to help those poor souls in our prisons."

"That's only a cover to disguise the money he is getting from other dubious sources."

"What other sources?" She retorted. "He has set up a business as a Corn Merchant, what is wrong with that?"

"The money he is getting is from smuggling, not selling corn."

"That's a lie. What evidence do you have?"

"I can't prove it yet but he is playing a dangerous game which could bring about his downfall. You must not get involved, I beg you as a friend and a suitor who worshipped the ground you walked on ever since we were children, don't let him ruin your life."

"Jan, I have always been fond of you and I know you of me but on this matter you have no proof. As to my heart, our relationship could never develop beyond friends but I do respect your advice and I will think on it. Now I must return to the Ball."

Jan placed his hands on her bare shoulders and kissed her gently on the mouth. She hesitated for a moment but did not back away. He drew her close in a lasting embrace. Her mouth yielded to his persuasive tongue and she found herself powerless to stop the passion that swept over her.

"You always could make me do things I was unable to control," she gasped softly.

His hand snaked delicately under the bodice of her evening dress and gently caressed the milk white breasts that stood hard and erect. Her body shivered unable to resist the desire she felt for this dangerous young man who had always had the ability to take her to places she didn't want to go.

The Ball finished at three o'clock. The guests who had wined and dined well left in subdued order. Some were a shade worse for wear including Jan and his three companions but, despise the uncomfortable nature of the chaise, they all slept soundly until a faint glimmer of light appeared over the sea to coincide with their arrival at Prussia Cove.

Once inside Bessies, the two couples crawled gratefully to their rooms and were quickly asleep. It was not until a week later that Meg overcame her curiosity and asked Jan if he had spoken to Anna at the Ball. She had dropped subtle hints but he had refused to be drawn.

"Yes," he replied and that was all he said.

CHAPTER 15

Spring was gradually giving way to summer. The daffodils, which flowered early in Cornwall's mild climate, had disappeared paving the way for the yellow gorse and the mauve heather that clung to the weather beaten hill tops to tell their message of warmer times to come. Predictably the lot of the miners was still grave. Jan had continued to deliver speeches all over the county spreading his gospel as far as Botallack and St. Austell but little seemed to come of it.

One early June morning, John Carter arrived at the Ship and Castle and asked if he might join him on a visit he was making to the miners of St. Day. Jan readily agreed. He had not been to that particular area before although he had been close when he visited Wheal Cupid. He was glad of the company.

It was a magnificent sun-drenched afternoon. The air was crystal clear and made the grimness of winter seem a distant memory. John was in good spirits laughing and joking all the way up the hill out of Falmouth. Jan responded with alacrity, he had been feeling the familiar pangs of frustration again, no matter what he said in public, nothing seemed to get done. Even the blackened, soot-stained chimneys of the knackt bals they passed did nothing to dampen their spirits.

They reached St. Day at five o'clock and had little difficulty in finding the St. Day Inn where they were welcomed by Captain Treventon, who had ridden over from Wheal Cupid earlier to arrange food and drink for his distinguished guest.

The Captain and John Carter had only met face to face once although their business dealings had been operating for a number of years.

"Pleasure to have you along Mr. Carter," he boomed and grasped John's hand. "'Tis a big one tonight, Jan, all the miners from Gwennap and Redruth are coming."

Jan raised his eyebrows.

"Unusual, normally a St Day man would think the best thing about Gwennap is the road out."

"They're all bound by a common cause now. 'Tis a funny thing, they'll fight till they drop over tuppence or an insult but if anything happens underground they're at the pithead ready to lay down their life for their fellow miner."

The three men consumed a large portion of barley bread and a quantity of beer that the Landlord had kept to perfection whilst discussing the best strategies to make those outside the mining community aware of the problems in the heartland of Cornwall. As the meal progressed John Carter became progressively more subdued. Jan put it down to being so far from the sea and thought nothing more about it.

The meeting was to be held on the side of a hill that overlooked the village. It was well chosen, a natural depression in the ground allowed the speaker to look down on his audience and ensure that everyone present could hear what was being said. By now the Captain and Jan had established a regular pattern. They would take up their positions early and once the Captain thought there were enough people present, he would call them to order and set the scene for Jan to unleash his unique brand of oratory. The Captain was a shrewd man. He gave Jan his head at these gatherings knowing that his words came from the heart, engendering a wild passion that would fire the flames of hope for those desperate for a better life. Jan knew he had a gift and, so far, the miners had listened, but the longer he kept preaching meaningless words that were not backed up with results, the more disillusioned the miners would become.

As it was a pleasant evening they left the Inn earlier than usual anticipating a good turn- out. They were not mistaken. A newspaper report later estimated a crowd of 25,000 had gathered to listen to the speakers, nearly a quarter of the total population of the area.

John Carter sat on the grass ledge next to Jan and surveyed the scene below. He knew that Jan drew big crowds but this was something special.

Both the Captain and Jan felt it. There was something different about the hordes gathering below. There was none of the usual noise and disorder they had come to expect from a group of undisciplined miners. This evening they were silent and unmoving. Jan did not like it and even, the phlegmatic Captain Treventon was uneasy.

"Best take it easy tonight, Jan. I don't like the mood they're in – 'taint natural for 'em all to be stood as quiet as this."

"The calm before the storm," murmured John to himself as he surveyed the droves of unsmiling, desperate faces that stretched out before him.

The Captain started the build up slowly for fear of inciting the miner's beyond a point he was unable to control. The crowd stood listening patiently. Eventually Jan stood up and, after acknowledging the cheers, launched into another of his passionate speeches.

"Friends, we are getting to the end of our tether. For seven months I have been pleading, cajoling and even begging those with money and influence to help your good selves from reaching the point of starvation. And what has been the result? Nothing."

He paused to let the effect of his words sink in to the silent listeners.

"Every day you go down in the gigs, spend eight hours working with picks and shovels. You come up again satisfied that you have done an honest day's work for King and Country. But what then? You walk home to a house starved of food, where you find your wives in tears and your children pleading for sustenance to satisfy the gnawing pangs of hunger that tear at their swollen bellies."

Murmurs of agreement filtered around the hillside.

"It is not enough to expect a man to live and work on barley bread and limpets, all we ask for is that enough food is brought to Cornwall so that we can live a proper healthy life. That is the right of every working man in this County."

At this juncture, John Carter, who had been listening intently to what Jan had to say, sprang to his feet and shouted,

"I know where there is enough food to feed all of you and it is in this County. There is enough Corn in the warehouses on Falmouth quay to feed all of Camborne and Redruth.

Corn, lots of it. Enough to take away the pangs of hunger that haunt your existence."

Jan tried to restrain him but John Carter was having none of it. His eyes were wild and the glint of anticipation flowed from his whole body. He was like a man possessed by the Devil and neither Jan nor Captain Treventon had the power to stop him

"If the food is there why don't we take it?" He yelled.

Shouts of approval rang out in sporadic outbursts of support, growing louder all the time.

"The corn belongs to the Corn Merchants who would rather sell their bushels abroad at a greater price than keep it for the likes of us, their own kind. I say, let's march on Falmouth and take what is rightly ours. It was grown on Cornish soil so it belongs to us."

The tiny pockets of support for John's words had now become an avalanche as the Cornish miners' voices rose as one. They were at fever pitch, hanging on every utterance from the King of Prussia.

Jan glanced at Captain Treventon. He was ashen.

"Does he know what he is doing, Jan?" The Captain said desperately. "He'll not be able to control 'em now."

Jan shrugged his shoulders.

"He knows that more than you or I, but it is more than my life's worth to stop him now."

John Carter was holding forth with a stream of eloquent words that had the multitude near to hysteria.

"So I say my friends follow the King of Prussia and we will get justice."

At the mention of this, the crowd went berserk. The King of Prussia? Here in St. Day? It was like a dream come true.

"Let us join together and take what is rightfully ours. Are you with me?"

The hordes of miners waved their fists in the air and roared their support. John Carter leapt off the granite boulder on which he was standing and yelled,

"Falmouth! That's where we go, follow me."

Caught up in the euphoria John Carter had created, the mass of humanity fell in behind clamouring to join the column as it snaked towards the seaport.

Jan turned to the good Captain who was watching in horror.

"Are you with us or no?"

The big man hesitated.

"Sir James warned me it might end like this. Mebbe 'tis a good thing, mebbe no, but sure as eggs is eggs I'll not miss this for the world."

It was a big decision for the stalwart Mine Captain who had never offended the law in his whole life. Grinning wildly they set off after the messianic figure of the King of Prussia as he led the march to Falmouth.

It was an orderly procession, those behind singing hymns taking care not to offend the folk on the way who, driven by curiosity, were peeking out from behind their shutters as they witnessed the crocodile of miners file past. The petty bickering and infighting prevalent in the mining towns was conspicuous by its absence as a common goal bound them together. There was no room for personal prejudice this was a matter of life or death.

Up front, John Carter walked briskly with Jan and the Captain at his side, occasionally turning round and yelling encouragement to those behind. Jan knew it was useless to stand in his way, John Carter knew exactly what he was doing. This was the chance he had been waiting for, ever since he left that stinking prison in Bodmin. He was not going to let it go now.

By the time the procession reached the outskirts of Penryn a casual glance back along the road showed that many of the original supporters had had second thoughts and turned back. Despite that, the number of flaming torches that pieced the night sky numbered over a thousand, each one convinced that this was the only course of action left open to them if they were to survive.

John called a halt at the crossroads.

"Some of you have families and children to think of, no one will think any the worse of you if you decide to turn back. You have done more than your share to support the night's actions. You can feel proud that you have been part of something that will help the miners' cause. Those who vote to stay- we march on to the warehouses on Custom House Quay."

Jan had heard a similar speech before in Bessies the day after he had met the King of Prussia for the first time. He knew that John Carter had hi-jacked the meeting and had encouraged the miners to pursue a path that was highly dangerous for all those involved but as he looked around not one man chose to leave the procession.

It was midnight when the miners reached the town. John called a halt at the Moor, it being the most convenient place in which to address such a large gathering.

"Now men, we are in a strange town, our quarrel is not with the gentle and kind folk who live here. We must respect their property and concentrate on the task which we have marched eight miles to accomplish."

A murmur of agreement came from the resolute miners.

"Tell us where the corn is, that's what we're here for," someone shouted from the darkness.

"Aye, we don't want nuthin with Fal folk, just show us the Warehouses," said another.

"You'll find them soon enough," John Carter replied reassuringly. "But first we must secure the transport on which to convey the corn back to our homes."

At that moment, from behind a group of buildings on the opposite side of the Moor, a group of men emerged leading a string of donkeys.

Jan immediately picked up the unmistakable gait of Henry Carter and the towering figure of Jake Tanna. He felt a lump rise in his throat as he watched the miners greet the men from Prussia Cove with obvious delight.

"So, he planned this all along," thought Jan to himself unable to stop his face breaking into an incredulous smile. He suspected John was up to something, this had been a meticulously planned operation designed to incite the miners to riot and at the same time, deal a bloody nose to the Merchant stockpiling his corn with a view to making scandalous profits. He did not have to think hard to know who that was.

It was a touching sight, seafaring men standing shoulder to shoulder with the rugged men who plied their trade a thousand feet below where they stood. Despite the keen interest the men from Prussia Cove had in the eventual outcome, Jan had no doubts that the solidarity for the miners' cause would have been there anyway.

"Now you know Jan," John Carter said evenly. "I'm sorry if I duped you but it was the only way, I had to be sure the miners would come. You and the Captain did a fine job in controlling the crowd but I needed the opposite. A riot is the only way these starving people can make those in Government sit up and take notice."

Jan couldn't find it in his heart to disagree. He had done all he could to stir the pot but it was the charisma of the King of Prussia that had brought it to boiling point. What happened now was in the hands of the miners.

"You have guessed who owns the Warehouses?"

"Peter Pendennis?"

"Yes, but revenge is not the only reason. These men are starving, I was like that once, so thin my ribs punctured the skin. The time has come for the talking to stop. Actions will speak louder than words this night."

"What will happen to you and I and of course, the good Captain, we will be the ones held responsible?"

John frowned.

"There is a risk but I have known you long enough to know that it will be a risk worth taking. This is a matter of life and death, if those miners do not get enough food we shall be digging graves for thousands of these unfortunate souls."

He waved his arm expansively and Jan could see the intense determination on the dark faces that were waiting patiently for the King of Prussia's next order. Jan smiled in the darkness, he had spent many years trying to control his own impulsiveness and now it was ironic that he was the one trying to be rational and cautious.

"What now, King of Prussia?" Asked Jan jokingly, his mind made up.

"To the Warehouses, Jan, and to hell with the consequences."

News of the invasion had reached Falmouth earlier in the evening and a message had been hurriedly dispatched to the Garrison on Pendennis point. A detachment of fifty soldiers was detailed to march into town and quell the riot. Their orders were to proceed to Custom House Quay and assemble in front of the warehouses, rifles at the ready.

It was a tense few minutes for the soldiers as they waited in the dark listening to the sounds of tramping feet as they got closer to the quayside. It was a spine-tingling period that tested their courage to their limit.

"Fix bayonets!" The order came from the Lieutenant of the Guard resplendent in his red coat and polished brass buttons. The noise of cold steel rang out around the harbour.

The first of the miners came round the corner and stopped dead as they saw the row of muskets pointing at them, forty yards away.

John Carter forced himself to the front.

"Halt!" The command rang out like a pistol shot. "Halt! Or my men open fire."

An uneasy silence reigned. Both sides unsure what to do next. It was John Carter who spoke first.

"Come now, Lieutenant, we only want what is rightfully ours."

The tension eased for a second.

"If you are the spokesman for this rabble, sir, I suggest you order them back to where they came from."

An angry murmur came from those men close enough to hear. The patronising tone and arrogant manner did nothing to endear the Lieutenant to the group of starving miners.

"I fear, sir, I cannot do that. These men are starving they need food and that food is inside those warehouses."

As he spoke, the weight of the crowd behind was slowly pushing John towards the row of fixed bayonets. The Lieutenant looked uneasily at the advancing crowd, there were far more than he had been led to believe.

"Do not advance another pace," he commanded. "I do not want to tell my men to shoot."

Still the miners edged forward, pushed by those at the rear, anxious to hear what was going on.

"Fire!"

The Lieutenant's order was followed by a devastating wall of lead that whistled over the heads of the demonstrators. Bullets screamed and ricocheted around the granite walls wining dangerously close to those on the quayside. The pushing stopped.

"Next time, my men will shoot to kill."

The Lieutenant's command was high and shrill, aware that his next order could bring about certain death to those in the front line.

The smell of acrid powder mingled with the dense smoke from the flaming torches, lending a macabre backcloth to the scenes on the waterfront.

Jan grasping the situation, pleaded desperately to the soldiers.

"It's me, Jan Pendray," he yelled as they stood on one knee waiting for the next lethal order.

"Jan Pendray," he repeated. "You all know me. George Penhaligon? Joseph Meneer? Parkie Penrose? You're all there I can see you. I have known you all my life, not one of you would dream of raising a gun to a fellow Cornishman. I ask you as friends, let these men pass. They are half crazed with hunger and will not harm anyone."

Jan's words struck home with the nervous row of soldiers, no amount of military training could eradicate their feelings for those who shared a common bond.

The pressure from behind was inching them forward again.

"Don't say I haven't warned you." The Lieutenant screamed. "Open fire!"

At that moment, Jan, seized the moment and rushed towards the line of muskets. His words had produced uncertainty in the ranks, it was enough.

The miners, seeing the line breached, rushed forward as the second volley of shots ploughed into the charging mass of humanity.

Screams of pain echoed around the narrow space as the bullets seared through those unfortunate enough to be in the line of fire. But now there was a way through. The miners trampled mercilessly over the hapless soldiers who were outnumbered by twenty to one.

John Carter was quick to seize the opportunity Jan had created and was through the line in an instant, with the weight of the miners behind him, the old wooden doors creaked and eventually fell. The first miners to tumble inside stared in amazement. Piled up to the ceiling was row upon row of sacks filled to the brim with precious corn.

John tried to organise a semblance of order but it was hopeless, each miner was mesmerised by the mountains of grain that would save them from certain starvation. However, with the arrival of the mules and the cajoling of Henry Carter with help from the rest of the smugglers, sanity was restored. Once they started loading John Carter left them to it and went in search of Jan.

The first charge through the barrier of muskets had left Jan with a gaping wound to his arm that was pumping blood at an alarming rate. He had managed to struggle to the side of the warehouse and avoid being trampled to death by the eager looters behind but he was weakening fast. John found him slumped against a warehouse wall.

"Jan, you're hurt."

"It's only a cut," he replied feebly trying to get up.

"That's no cut, Jan," John replied slowly, noting the blood that was congealing on the inside of his jacket.

"Can you walk?"

"I think so."

John helped him to his feet and slinging a powerful arm under his shoulder, he half carried Jan up a side alley away from the mayhem that had descended on the quayside. By the time they had reached the main street Jan had lost a lot of blood and was barely conscious. John Carter, spurred on by the proximity of the Ship and Castle, lifted his patient onto his shoulders and staggered forward.

Meg, like many other residents, was on the street wondering what was going on. When she saw John Carter, she stifled a scream and helped him into the Inn.

She knew the body slumped on his back was Jan. Quickly she took charge of the situation. Fetching a carving knife from the kitchen, she cut the material from his shoulder and exposed the wound that was still gushing blood like a stirrup pump. It was clear that Jan was in a bad way, his face was drained of colour and his eyes were staring hauntingly into space, unaware of where he was. Valiantly Meg applied a tourniquet to the nine inch wound, fighting back the tears as she saw how desperate the situation was for her man.

Having carried Jan to the upstairs room, John Carter had to leave.

"Can you manage, Meg? I have to go back."

Meg gave him a grim smile.

"Go, John I will look after Jan, your task is not finished yet. God go with you."

She kissed him on the cheek and waved him out of the room.

As he was leaving he said, "Jan's a lucky man to have a woman like you, perhaps one day he will come to realise it."

Meg gave a thin smile and returned to bathing Jan's wound as best she could.

John retraced his path back to the quay. He had been gone thirty minutes but already he could sense the mood of the miners had changed. Beforehand they had been restrained and controlled. Now they were rapidly turning into an unruly mob. The reason for the turnabout was plain to see. Not only had the miners discovered the corn but also a large consignment of illicit liquor buried carefully beneath the sacks. It had been too much of a temptation. They had laid into the drink and were now dangerously drunk.

Henry Carter had tried to prevent them but he was hopelessly outnumbered. Unlike the fierce discipline binding the Prussia Cove smugglers, these men were mavericks living for the day. Most of them had never tasted anything more than the cheap gin sold in the Kiddliwinks, so fine French brandy was Manna from Heaven.

John was quick to assess the situation.

"Round up the men, let's get out of here before reinforcements come from the garrison."

With a speed born out of circumstance, the smugglers led the fully laden mules away from the quay taking care to avoid the numerous bodies that lay in their path. Once up the narrow alleyways they reached the main street where the going was easier. Accompanied by voluminous curses the mules moved painfully slowly away from the chaos that reigned down by the water.

John was relieved to see the giant figure of Captain Treventon emerge from the shadows. Fortunately he was sober.

"What of Jan?" He asked anxiously.

"He's hurt but he is in good hands. Your job is to see that these mules get to Redruth and the corn is dispersed as quickly as possible."

John's voice was terse.

The giant Captain nodded curtly.

"I will do that but it won't be easy. You cannot expect miners to follow your code. They were whipped into a frenzy by your words and now the drink..."

"You were aware of the risks," snapped John. "Now they are putting the lives of my men at risk."

The Mine Captain drew himself up to his full height, bristling at John Carter's remarks.

"It was you who started all this, you knew what you were doing right from the start. You used the miners to further your desire for revenge. I'll do what I can to get the corn to those who need it but I won't thank you for it."

They were walking beside the mules tugging the reluctant animals up the hill towards Penryn. After much cursing and cajoling the smugglers, aided by Jonas Treventon and a few miners who had remained sober, they reached the top of the hill overlooking Lanner.

John turned to the Mine Captain.

"I'm sorry we do not see eye to eye on this, Captain. Now my men are out of danger I will return and see if there is anything I can do."

Treventon shook his head sadly.

"You don't see it, do you? You are not dealing with a small band of well-disciplined smugglers. Those men left in Falmouth are a bunch of ill-bred vagabonds who would stick a knife in yer back as soon as look at 'ee. It will take more than your sea-faring ways to stop 'em now."

For the first time John Carter's confident mask slipped a fraction.

"What do you suggest then, Captain?"

"Leave 'em be. Get out of the area afore it's too late."

John Carter hesitated as he weighed up the situation. If only there had been corn and no liquor in the warehouse the operation would have been completed successfully by now.

"No," he said finally. "You are right, I started it so I must finish it. I am going back to Falmouth."

The men from Prussia Cove knew it was useless to argue, so, with a final volley of instructions to his men, John Carter turned on his heel and headed back to the town.

Setting off at a steady trot, he reached the quay as the reinforcements from the Garrison arrived. Everywhere there were miners fighting, the sense of unity lost in a haze of drink. Old enmities between the mining villages were being sorted out amongst the debris that littered the harbour side, they were incapable of appreciating the danger they were in. A volley of shots from the reinforcements sent bullets ricocheting off the walls in a deadly spray of lead.

John Carter stood in a secluded alleyway and watched in horror. Many of those shot were too drunk to feel the pain, dying in a pool of blood where, five minutes earlier, they had sunk in a pool of Brandy. They had no chance, round after round were fired into the mass of writhing humanity who could offer no resistance to the hail of bullets.

John Carter sank further into the shadows aghast at what he had witnessed. Not one miner left on the quay escaped the deadly missives delivered from the rows of straight-barrelled muskets.

In ten minutes it was all over. All that could be heard was the pitiful groans from the injured as the pain pierced the cocoon of alcohol. They had been butchered by their own kind all for the want of providing enough food to feed their community. John Carter stood transfixed, the smell of cordite and the sight before his eyes made him violently sick.

"Not this!" He cried. "Nothing could be worth this."

Tears rolled down his cheeks as he wandered in a dream, listening to the cries and watching those still alive trying valiantly to help those whose cause was beyond redemption.

Suddenly someone grabbed him by the arm.

"Get out of here, there's nothing for you to do here."

John Carter appeared not to hear.

"For God's sake, man, you've done your job, 'tis not for you to stay. If they catch you, you'll swing for sure."

John turned to face the miner.

"Maybe I deserve to hang. I have driven all of you to disaster."

"No one in the mining towns will blame you for this. It had to happen sooner or later. Maybe someone will listen now."

"No, I have got to take the blame for this. It will be on my conscience until the day I die. Never again will I let my impulsiveness dictate my actions."

"Well, have it your way but go now afore it's too late."

The nameless miner pushed John away from the quay.

"What of the wounded?" He asked over his shoulder.

"Don't 'ee fret over they, my beauty, us miners can look after ourselves – we'll manage."

With one last look at the ghastly sight before him, John reluctantly turned away.

It was only a minute to the Ship and Castle. Meg responded to his knocking and let him in, swiftly locking the door behind him.

"What's happened?" she asked anxiously. "I heard the shooting, is it bad?"

"A bloody massacre," he replied bitterly. They didn't stand a chance. I never thought I would see the day when Cornishmen would raise powder to fellow Cornishmen."

Meg saw the look on John's face.

"Sit down and drink this."

She handed him a tumbler full of rum.

He gulped it down, the fire catching the back of his throat. It helped ease the sickness he felt in the pit of his stomach.

"How's Jan?"

"He's asleep. He has lost a lot of blood. It will take time for him to recover."

Meg spoke in soft tones, her face pallid and drawn. For the first time that night, her self-control began to waver.

"Come on, Meg, don't crack now, Jan needs you more than ever."

John was regaining some of his composure.

"Once daylight comes, the Militia will be out in force. They will be searching everywhere for us. We have to move Jan to a safer place."

"No!" Meg cried. "If we move him he will die."

"If he stays here he will die on the end of a rope. This will be the first place they will search."

Meg's face was white.

"Where can we go then?" She wailed.

"I did know some merchants in Penryn who owe me a favour, but I cannot guarantee that their heads would not be turned by the sight of gold coins."

They were so engrossed in their deliberations they did not hear the door open.

"Sir James St, Aubyne will help."

They wheeled round instantly.

"Jan!" Meg gasped. "You should be in bed."

"I'm alright, help me to the sofa."

Meg rushed to his side and guided him across the room.

"He lives at Tregothnan on the Fal near Truro. If we can get there all our problems..." His voice drifted away as he collapsed on the sofa.

"Jan!" Meg cried. "What a fool, what a stubborn fool."

She brushed his hair back and held his head in her arms.

"Best leave him here for the moment, Meg, he's very weak. He will need all the rest he can get if we are to make it to Tregothnan."

Meg was distraught, she knew that staying at the Ship and Castle was madness but she feared Jan would not survive the journey. John read her thoughts.

"Meg, the alternative is the gallows. Men died out there tonight and we will be held responsible."

She did not reply, busying herself by making Jan as comfortable as possible. When she stood up, John Carter had gone. It was a traumatic moment for her. She knew John was right, it was impossible for them to stay, but the thought of moving Jan in his present condition was tantamount to murder. It was a journey of seven miles on a road that was pitted with holes.

She placed her head in her hands and cried. John Carter who had been gone barely an hour, found her still sitting next to the sleeping Jan. Some of the old sparkle was back although he still found it impossible to eradicate the events from the night from his mind.

"Come on Meg, we have got to go."

He grabbed her gently by her shoulder and levered her up.

"We can't move him he will never stand the journey. The road is terrible," she wailed.

"Don't worry, we only have to get him to the wharf."

"What wharf?"

"The wharf by the St. Mawes ferry, I've got a boat."

Meg's eyes lit up.

"Of course, the lands of Tregothnan stretch right down to the river Fal, we don't have to go by road."

Suddenly she was transformed. The hopelessness of their position was banished and the possibility of escape generated a feverish round of activity. John sighed with relief, he needed her to be positive if he was to engineer a successful departure.

"'Tis only a small rowing boat so we cannot take anything with us. We must go now."

They struggled to carry the semi-conscious Jan out of the Inn and down the alley to the quay. There were still a few miners about, some sober enough to drag themselves away from the waterfront in the hope that the inhabitants of the town would take pity on them. Many of the town folk did. They were quick to condemn the Militia for firing on their own flesh and blood.

John Carter was surprised that the Militia had melted away. According to one witness, they were so horrified by the carnage their first volley of shots had caused, it had forced the commanding officer to order them back to the Garrison to avoid further bloodshed. John Carter was relieved. They still had a slim chance.

The tiny rowing boat was still moored by the jetty. John staggered down the stone steps carrying Jan over his shoulder. Meg, giving furtive glances behind, followed. The steps were covered with slimy, green seaweed making it difficult to manoeuvre Jan into the boat without capsizing. Eventually they got the prone figure into the stern and covered him with an old blanket Meg had grabbed as she left the Inn.

John untied the mooring rope and prepared to take the oars.

"Well, Meg, back to the Inn before you catch cold, I can manage from here."

Meg shook her head vehemently.

"No, I am coming with you."

John threw his hands in the air.

"The boat won't take three of us."

"Yes it will. I've been out in smaller boats than this and we have had three up."

John Carter gave her a look of exasperation but he knew arguing was useless.

"O.K. if that's the way you want it, we are in God's hands."

She clambered aboard and the water level rose ominously until the gentle wave from the bow splashed into the tiny dinghy. Gingerly John edged the craft away from the wall and into the harbour. The first glimmer of dawn was shimmering on the horizon as John pulled powerfully on the oars and made a course across the harbour. Meg had lied, she had never been in a boat this small but the thought of being left behind while Jan suffered a mortal fate was too much to bear, if they drowned, so be it, at least she was with the man she loved.

John realising that any deviation would spell certain disaster, settled into an easy rhythm using his many years of seamanship to ensure that the boat remained on an even keel. Meg sat in the stern, Jan's head resting on her lap. In her other hand she held a wooden cup, intermittently she would lean forward and scoop out the water that accumulated in the bottom of the boat.

John could not take his mind away from the massacre, in the cold light of day his impetuosity had caused it, whichever way he looked at it, he kept coming to the conclusion that it was his fault. Even if there had not been any of Pendennis's contraband in the warehouses, the miners would have created a riot off their own backs. That volume of corn was more than they had ever seen in their lives. They were bound to feel a deep resentment.

Fortunately the water in the bay was calm and John was able to row smoothly keeping the water splash to a minimum. In any other situation the trip would have been hugely enjoyable. It was John who broke the silence.

"Is that it, over there?"

He had been rowing steadily for an hour, making good use of the tide that was pushing them towards the opposite side of the River Fal.

Meg turned slowly.

"No, that is Loe Beach, we must get further up river."

John grimaced and redoubled his efforts causing the ripple from the bow to send fine sprays of water into the dinghy.

The Tregothnan Estate stretched down to the foreshore a few miles upstream from Devoran. By the time they spotted the small jetty and the big mansion in the background, the sun was beginning to climb high in the sky. John was exhausted, he had rowed from Falmouth without a break, great welts on his palms had burst and the blood mingled with the stinging salt water causing severe pain. He did not complain, doggedly setting his mind on the wooden platform that stretched out into the river in the distance.

At last, after what seemed an interminable time, Meg who had watched the jetty grow steadily larger, reached out and guided the boat alongside the quay. Thankfully, John pulled in the oars and slumped forward.

Meg let go of Jan and, gathering her skirt, she jumped nimbly onto the slatted balustrade. Without waiting she ran up the grass meadow in front of the mansion leaving John to recover from his exhausting trip.

There was no sign of life from the mansion. She dashed around to the front of the building and tugged vigorously on the bell sash outside the front door. She heard a loud jangling from inside but no response. She tugged again, praying silently that the building was occupied. On the third ring she heard the bolt being drawn back. The door eased open and a head poked out.

"What do you want?" The Butler was unable to keep the surliness from his voice.

"I must see Sir James St. Aubyne at once, it is a matter of life and death."

"Master's still in bed." The reply was curt and uncompromising.

At that point Meg recognised a familiar voice.

"Let the person in Troups, it must be important to call at this hour... Why, the mistress of the Ship and Castle."

Sir James stood there dressed in a long, silk cloak and wearing a pair of moccasin slippers.

"Sir James, Jan is gravely ill. John Carter and I have brought him over from Falmouth by boat. May we bring him in?"

Sir James's reaction was immediate.

"Troups, get two others and go down to the jetty at once."

Relief poured from Meg like a fountain.

"Thankyou, Sir James, from the bottom of my heart."

She did not know Sir James well enough to have predicted his reaction. Indeed, she had been sceptical about John's plan from the beginning. It was the lack of an alternative that forced her to go along with it.

At that moment, Sir James was joined by a tall, elegant lady with wispy, grey hair. She was evidently his wife. When she saw Jan, her face clouded in genuine concern. She immediately sprang into action.

"I will prepare a room for the wounded one at once. Perhaps you would like to help."

Meg felt tears of gratitude sting her eyes.

"You are so kind, Lady St. Aubyne."

She smiled at the young girl and took her arm reassuringly.

"Don't you worry. He will be well cared for."

By the time the men had staggered up the stairs, Lady St Aubyne and Meg had made up a bed and prepared a fresh set of bandages for Jan's wounded shoulder. Lady St Aubyne was a wonder. With a minimum of fuss she organised everything down to the last detail leaving Meg in awe of such a kind and considerate lady. Together they laid the delirious Jan on the bed and set about peeling away the blood-soaked linen. It was a mess but Lady St Aubyne assured Meg, the wound was not yet infected. Given time and rest there was a good chance that Jan would recover.

Downstairs, having soaked his hands in warm water John Carter was in deep conversation with Sir James.

"You are safe enough here for the time being but for how long, I cannot say. I have given orders for the dinghy to be sunk and I can trust my servants not to say a word, but, as you know, Cornwall has a habit of unearthing one's most precious secrets, however hard you try to conceal them."

"I do appreciate your kindness Sir James and I speak for Meg and Jan as well. It was Jan's idea to come to you, at the time it was the only course left open to us."

"That does not surprise me," Sir James smiled. "Jan has done a lot for the miner without him really knowing it. He always knew it was I who set him up for the job in the first place. Now, tell me what happened last night."

It was the question John had been dreading. He coughed nervously acutely aware of his Lordship's steady gaze. He knew it was impossible to lie so he launched into a detailed account of the night's events leaving nothing out and including his own sorry contribution to the tragic events.

Sir James listened gravely. He let John tell the events without interruption and when he had finished his reaction was not what John had expected.

"I knew it would have to come to this sooner or later. Don't blame yourself, I agree you let revenge colour your judgement but it was a mere catalyst. The riot was the consequence of many years of poverty and near starvation. Jan knew he was sitting on top of a powder keg. You provided the one spark. I was hoping it would come earlier so the miners could avoid starvation. I do not approve of men being shot in cold blood but we live in an age that cares little for those less fortunate than ourselves. It takes an event like this to make people sit up and listen."

John Carter, although still stricken with conscience, was relieved to hear what Sir James had to say. He was learning that it was true what they said about Lord St. Aubyne's integrity and he was glad to have his endorsement.

"Sir James, there is one more favour I would like to ask of you, if I may."

Sir James nodded unable to disguise the twinkle in his eye.

"Go ahead, I can but listen."

"I need to send word to my brother that I am still alive and, if possible fix a meeting. Could this be arranged?"

"I don't see why not. I will send a man at once. A meeting here at Tregothnan would be the safest plan."

John's relief was tangible.

"Thank you, Sir James. I appreciate the risk you are taking."

Sir James sighed and clasped John's hand with genuine warmth.

"Mr. Carter, for what you have done for the miner in Cornwall this night, it is a privilege to be of assistance."

John Carter was moved. Instead of condemnation, here was a pillar of society actually clasping his hand in friendship.

By this time the sun was well up in a cloudless sky giving a feeling of peace and tranquillity far removed from the unhappy events of the previous night.

The stillness was suddenly shattered by the sound of hooves on the gravel drive outside. John, who had gone to join Meg in the bedroom, leapt up and went to the window. Beneath him were five uniformed men of the Militia. He shrank back behind the heavy curtains and stood there with bated breath.

Sir James answered the door himself. A conversation followed that John was unable to hear. As time went on he became more anxious, what if he had misread Sir James' intentions?

Eventually a lull occurred in the conversation and John risked a further peek. He was just in time to see the erect figure of Sir James St Aubyne mount a saddled horse and follow the five Militiamen down the drive. Their destination was a mystery.

John sat back on the window seat lost in thought. Supposing he had turned against them, what would happen? There would be little hope for Jan and only marginally more for Meg and himself. Meg left the bedside when she heard the horses leave and watched them go. As if she was reading John's thoughts she said firmly:

"We can trust Sir James, he will not let us down."

John nodded slowly. He was annoyed with himself for even considering the possibility that Sir James would turn them in. He had already risked a great deal on their behalf.

"How is Jan?" He asked turning his attentions to the motionless figure on the bed.

"No change. Lady St Aubyne thinks that he will recover but it will take time. She is a kind woman and would not say things she did not mean."

John agreed. "I have heard many tales about her. She is a living legend in these parts. No one knows where she came from. Rumour has it she was a bal maiden from down Wheal Taphouse way, a daughter of a miner so they say. Anyway she has done well for herself and not because she has been lucky enough to marry into the aristocracy. It would not surprise me if a large part of Sir James's mining interests are under her watchful eye."

"She is a clever woman, maybe I will be like her one day."

John laughed.

"Perhaps one day, but right now your job is to see that Jan gets better. I think that is the most important thing in your life if I am not mistaken."

Meg blushed.

"I have never told anyone this John, my late husband died when I was twenty leaving me to run the Ship and Castle on my own. For two years I did not look at another man, partly out of respect and partly because I loved my husband despite what the old gossips might have said. Then Jan came along. Right away I knew this was different. Once I had seen and talked to him I could do nothing to keep him out of my thoughts. I tried to forget him, I knew he was in love with Anna and didn't care for me in the same way but I couldn't stop myself. I love him."

John listened attentively.

"Do you love him more than your late husband?"

"It is a different kind of love. As my late husband was forty years older than me, he found ways to my heart by kindness and devotion With Jan we are from the same generation, we are both strong willed and he possesses a reckless streak. He often hurts me without knowing it. Then he becomes repentant and regrets what he has done."

John smiled at the young girl who had such a heavy burden thrust upon her slender shoulders at such an early age.

"Meg, if you have a love which you think is strong enough to withstand the test of time, hang on to it , encourage it and little by little you will find that the love you have nurtured will be transferred to the heart of your partner until he too, will be unable to live without it. There is nothing wrong in falling in love with Jan."

"But I do not know whether he loves me," she cried.

"Jan is more committed to you than he would care to admit. I know his heart has been wrung inside out by his feelings for Anna, but your love has a much better chance of success."

Meg sighed.

"Maybe you are right but I am not sure. He saw Anna at the Ball in Penzance but he would not say what passed between them."

"Perhaps he will when he is ready. Don't give up hope, once Jan makes up his mind he will take no other and he will become a devoted and trustworthy consort."

"I do hope so, John. Thank you for listening."

She leant forward and kissed him on the cheek.

"A curse on that Jan Pendray," he said smiling. "He doesn't know how lucky he is."

With that he got up and left them alone in the bedroom.

It was nightfall when Sir James returned. John, who had kept a wary ear to the ground, was relieved to note that only one set of hooves could be heard crunching on the gravel outside.

Sir James' face was grave. He poured them both a stiff drink and sat down in the drawing room.

"The five Militia, who called this morning, had been chasing a group of men from Falmouth. They believed they had been looting a warehouse on the quay."

"That could have been my brother," prompted John quickly.

"Anyway they got up close and fired a few rounds over their heads. The next thing they knew, a giant of a man who had detached himself from the group came charging at them with all the fury of the Devil. He unseated the first two riders and the other horses were on the point of stampeding."

"Good for him," John chipped in.

"Yes, it was a brave thing to do but sadly one of the Militia was able to reload his pistol and shot the man in the back of the head. Through his bravery the others were able to get away."

John was silent for a moment and then asked:

"Who was this brave man?"

With a long sigh Sir James replied heavily, "Captain Treventon."

John groaned. Although they had left on unsatisfactory terms he was visibly distraught. The Captain had long been an associate he had held in the highest esteem. He was a mountain amongst his mining friends who had the confident air of invincibility about him. He could not believe that the man was dead.

"I suppose he is dead?" John asked hopefully.

"Yes, that is why I went to Falmouth, to identify the body. One piece of good news though, it appears that his onslaught enabled your men to get away with the mules, so a few more lives will be saved from starvation."

It seemed poor compensation to John.

"His death will be a sad blow to the miners of Camborne and Redruth. They looked up to him, a leader they could trust."

John's voice trembled, this, more than the massacre of the previous night, grieved him greatly.

Sir James downed his whisky in one gulp.

"Yes, his presence will be greatly missed, he was a good Mine Captain who commanded the respect of all those under him."

He, too was finding it difficult to put his grief into words.

It was a long while before John could bring himself to ask what other news was forthcoming about the previous night. In response Sir James produced a broadsheet which he had tucked inside his waistcoat and handed it to John. It was a special edition printed by the Falmouth Packet giving a full account of the raid and its terrible aftermath. He read it through slowly. It appeared that his initial foreboding about the massacre had been exaggerated. According to the account, six men had died from gunshot wounds and a further two had drowned whilst under the influence of drink. It said nothing about how the illicit cargo had happened to be in the Warehouses or what happened to the bushels of corn. Instead it concentrated on why the miners were in Falmouth in the first place. However, at the bottom there was the statement he had been expecting.

During the rioting one of the Militia had been killed, allegedly by a knife wound to the throat. A warrant had been issued for the arrest of John Carter, King of Prussia, Jan Pendray and Captain Jonas Treventon. All three were accused of murder.

John put the sheet down his face grave. Now, nowhere was safe. The murder of a Militiaman was a crime against the King. No stone would be left unturned in the quest to find the culprits.

"It looks grim," John said heavily. "They will not let this rest."

Sir James nodded in agreement.

"Yes, you will not be safe in Cornwall. Even here at Tregothnan, I cannot guarantee your presence will not be discovered."

"You have already done more than enough to help us, Sir James, we cannot impose on you a moment longer. Tonight we move on."

A voice from over his shoulder replied.

"You will do no such thing."

It was Lady St. Aubyne who had entered the drawing room after changing Jan's bandages. "That boy upstairs cannot be moved. I will not allow you to go."

"Lady Aubyne, we are grateful for your kindness but you are harbouring two suspected killers. That makes you both accessories to murder. Not even your high station in the county would protect you."

"That is a risk we will take. We know you are not murderers. That is all that matters."

Lord St Aubyne winked at his wife but said nothing.

John shook his head, overcome with gratitude. He knew their escape was hopeless without their help.

"Well, perhaps, until my brother arrives. I will not countenance putting your lives in danger a moment longer than necessary."

"That's settled then," Sir James said with a note of finality. "Let us hope your brother gets the message and then we can set about forming a plan for the future."

They drank the remainder of the whisky in better heart.

"It is not all bad Mr. Carter," Sir James said as he drained his glass. "The authorities are beginning to take notice. Perhaps now they will see there is a problem. Your actions will not be in vain. The death of a few poor souls may be a small price to pay for the saving of a whole community."

John tried to agree but he found it impossible. The death of Captain Treventon weighed heavily on his conscience.

That night was one of the longest in Meg's life. She was oblivious to the dangerous events that were revolving around her, having eyes only for the prone figure which remained unconscious on the bed. She remained at his side constantly, mopping his sweating brow and whispering words of encouragement, hoping against hope, they were not falling on deaf ears. Sometimes he would mumble incoherently, Meg tried to understand but she could make little sense of his ramblings.

Towards morning, as the first glimmer of dawn appeared over the trees, Jan opened his eyes. He saw Meg sitting there and smiled. She tried to fight back the tears of relief but it was impossible, they rolled down her cheeks in an uncontrollable stream.

"I love you, Meg," he said weakly and immediately fell asleep.

Meg, still crying, held his hand tightly until the tears dried and for the first time for two days she slept.

CHAPTER 16

Henry Carter, once he had seen the heroic charge by Captain Treventon, knew that the convoy was safe. The seafaring men with grim handshakes all round, melted into the distance and left the distribution of the corn in the hands of the miners, their role in the monumental events of the night was done.

The men from Prussia Cove had prearranged dropping off points and it took only a short time to dispose of the mules and head back to the coast. The miners, at each rendezvous, were met by a line of patient women who whisked away the life-giving grain with an efficiency that was typical of their breeding.

When Henry Carter returned to the Cove, the messenger from Sir James was already there. He cursed his brother vehemently but acknowledged the request and dispatched the rider with the news that he would be at Tregothnan the following morning.

True to his word he arrived at the mansion at seven o'clock after a hard three hour ride. John and Sir James were already up and a huge breakfast with numerous cups of home brewed tea was ready and waiting. The three men remained in conference for the rest of the morning. Upstairs Jan was awake. Beside him lay the sleeping figure of Meg. He did not disturb her, he could tell from the lines etched onto her forehead that she had spared nothing to see that he recovered from his brush with death. He was vaguely aware of what had happened but large chunks seemed to be missing. During the period that he was unconscious, he had been aware of a struggle within himself. It was not merely a struggle for survival it was as though his mind was fighting to re-establish control of his body. It was a weird feeling. He stroked Meg's hair, careful not to wake her. He remembered what he had said and had no regrets. It was true. He had grown to love her although he had been reluctant to admit it. Any thoughts of Anna were lost in the realisation that Meg was unique, she had risked her life for him and threatened everything she owned just to be by his side. He could not believe how blind he had been.

His mind drifted away and on to the problems that they now faced. He was not aware of all that had occurred but he knew that their situation was serious. He tried to fathom it out but soon drifted back into a long, dreamless sleep.

"So it is all arranged, you must be at Gorran Haven ready to board at 12.00 tonight." It was Henry Carter speaking and it was clear that he had not been idle since receiving the message from his brother.

"The Queen of the Isles will hove to, on the evening tide for no more than an hour. The Captain will not wait a minute longer. If you do not make it, your fate will be in the hands of the Lord."

"You have done well, brother. I will see that we make the rendezvous."

"What of the woman?"

"I cannot say, I will have to ask her. She has a lot to lose if she sides with the King of Prussia."

The final plans for the flight from Cornwall were almost complete. Sir James had generously agreed to supply a horse and wagon to take them to the tiny port of Gorran Haven ten miles North-east of Truro.

The brothers shook hands and parted, their affection for each other preventing any prolonged words of farewell. From now on they were each in control of their own destinies. No longer could John Carter rely on the smuggling fraternity of Prussia Cove for support, he would have to shape his own destiny. He watched his brother saddle up and set off back to the cove, taking a deep breath he turned and went up the wide, carpeted stairs to the bedroom.

Meg was now awake, unaware that Jan had regained consciousness. She fussed around the bed straightening the sheets and feeling faintly annoyed with herself for falling asleep.

John entered the room softly.

"Ah! Meg I'm glad you are awake, I need to talk to you."

He sat down on the edge of the bed. Jan was still asleep.

"I told you he would be alright," he said looking at the colour that had returned to Jan's cheeks.

Meg smiled. "So far, so good. What is it you want to say?"

"My brother, Henry, has just left. We have been discussing what should be done. There is no chance of either of us staying in Cornwall without ending up on the end of a hangman's noose. Perhaps when the fuss dies down and the truth emerges we may be able to return. As things stand at the present, we have no alternative but to go."

"Where?"

"America."

Meg gasped.

"America?" She gasped. "The New World? That is thousands of miles away."

In common with most Cornish folk, a trip to Truro was the other end of the world, America was beyond comprehension.

"It is the only possibility, we are supposed to be at war with France and there is little hope of remaining undiscovered in England. With a little capital that I have arranged, we can take America by storm. Rumour has it that there are fortunes to be made for those who are prepared to work hard."

Meg sat back and let the full extent of the plan sink in. At first it had sounded ludicrous but after giving it some thought it did not sound so bad. There was just one point that troubled her.

"What will become of me?"

"That is what I wanted to talk to you about. There is room on board the vessel if you have a mind to come. It will not be an easy passage, I can make no promises but the berth is there if you want it."

Meg walked to the latticed window and stared out across the lawns to the waters of Falmouth Bay.

"It is a big opportunity that you are offering and I am very grateful. You have been a good friend to me and to Jan but what if I go and find that I am left alone with no friends and no prospects? It is different for a girl."

"There is no chance of that," the voice came from the other side of the bedroom. "If Meg does not come with us John Carter, then you are going on your own."

"Jan!" Meg gasped. "I did not know you were awake."

Jan smiled weakly and turned to his grinning friend. "We both go and that is the end of the matter."

Tears rolled down Meg's face as she rushed to his bedside.

"Do   you   really   mean   it,   Jan?"

"I have never been so certain of anything in my life. It took a brush with death to convince me. I love you Meg."

John Carter touched them both on the shoulder and left the bedroom. At least, something good had come out of the whole sorry saga.

Meg, her heart still aflutter, forced herself to concentrate on the business in hand. The Ship and Castle still remained and she did not want to see it go to rack and ruin. She wrote a note to be delivered to her sister in Constantine and another for Jamie Fidock that she gave to Sir James who promised to deliver them personally.

It was a sad farewell to Tregothnan for the three of them. The strength and fortitude of Lord and Lady St Aubyne had given them the will and determination to undertake such a hazardous journey. They had been happy for the short time they had been there and found it difficult to put into words the gratitude they felt. They need not have worried. Sir John was more than happy with what they had achieved. For the first time, questions would be asked in Parliament, the whole economy of the Industrial Revolution that was taking placed was based on the need for raw materials. If the miners could not produce them the startling progress that had been made over the last two decades, would grind to a halt. He knew that Peter Pendennis would be keeping a low profile and not be keen to press charges. The discovery of illicit cargo in the warehouses was a sure way to guarantee silence.

"Don't go away with a heavy heart," he said to the trio. "One day it will be safe for you to return and the miners will welcome you as their saviour."

He grasped John by the hand. "Go now," he said gruffly unable to prevent the shaking in his voice.

The three of them set off down the drive unable to look back. The whole house had turned out and stood around the Lord and Lady of the estate, waving their goodbyes in a genuine show of affection.

It was dark when they reached the Truro road, the only sound to break the silence was the gentle clip-clop of the pony and the crunching of the gravel as the cart bore them away from their refuge. It was Meg who found it the hardest. She had built up a steady business by dint of hard work. She was loathe to leave it behind. She had a special affection for the cantankerous customers and their individual foibles, they had stood by her when she lost her husband and now she was leaving without saying goodbye. It was solely the love for Jan that drove her forward, far stronger than the material possessions she was forced to abandon. Jan, although weak, read her thoughts and put his good arm around her. He did not need to say anything.

The road to Truro was deserted and they were able to make the outskirts of the town within the hour. There was no way of avoiding the town as it had grown up around the river Fal and the upper reaches had to be crossed. Their presence went unnoticed by the inhabitants who were only interested in frequenting the Inns and Taverns of the Stannery town.

"What do you think, Jan?" John enquired.

"I think it would be an admirable idea," he answered with a grin.

Meg was mystified, anxious to leave the town as soon as possible.

"What are you two talking about?"

"Well, seeing as this is the last chance we shall have to sample good Cornish ale ...."

"You must be mad!" Meg cried. " Not only are you ill but you are both wanted for murder."

It was no use they had made up their minds. Heaving the cart to a halt, John leapt off and helped Jan to the ground. Meg, still protesting vigorously, was forced to follow as they entered Ma Shaw's Inn, a drinking house with a reputation that had spread far beyond the area.

Their arrival attracted scant attention in the crowded bar. Jan sat in a corner while John ordered the drinks. Despite his weakness he was feeling good, maybe invigorated by the risk that they were taking.

It was the poster on the wall that first attracted Meg's attention. She leant forward and read the words:

£1000 reward for information leading to the whereabouts of John Carter alias The King of Prussia and Jan Pendray of Falmouth.

Meg was too far away to read the rest. She nudged Jan.

"Can you read that?"

Jan lent forward and grinned.

"We are worth more every day."

"How can you say that?" She whispered fiercely.

"Don't worry Meg, no one knows us here."

John returned with the drinks. He too, had read the poster including the small print.

"It appears our friend Sergeant Crowlas is back in the act. He has been placed in charge of the operation to bring us to justice. According to the poster, the owner of the warehouses has put up the thousand pounds, a fair sum. We must have hit him hard."

John gave a grim smile, he enjoyed giving Pendennis a bloody nose but it was tempered by the sad deaths that had occurred in the process.

"I'm surprised Pendennis wants the publicity," Jan replied. "Questions are bound to be asked about the French cargo."

John shrugged. "Smuggling has its way of silencing the loudest critics."

"I think we ought to go," Meg said getting more agitated with each sip.

Whether it was reckless bravado or a genuine desire to wring the last drop of comfort from the local brew, the two men ordered another. At last Meg got her wish and they got up to go. On the corner of the bar, hidden by a wooden pillar, a man watched them leave. Thoughtfully he downed his drink and, with a quick glance at the poster, he left the Inn. It was the man who had served Jan in the bank before he secured the services of Mr Hart.

Revived by the pleasant interlude, the three crossed the bridge over the river and set off towards the hamlet of Tresillian. The bell from the Monastery sounded the ninth hour. They had three hours to reach Gorran Haven.

Their route took them along the upper reaches of the Fal until they were far enough inland to cross onto the Roseland peninsula. The track was well-worn but narrow, so progress was slow. Numerous tree roots jolted the cart and it was not long before the pony was sweating profusely. Once out of Tresillian, away from the tree-lined river the going became easier. The earlier merriment was replaced by a grim realisation that their lives were about to change for ever.

Suddenly John Carter reined in the pony and listened. At first it was no more than a murmur which could have been caused by the whispering of the trees, but with every second it grew in intensity. There was no mistaking it, the dull thud of approaching horses.

"They are on to us," John said grimly. "No one around these parts would be riding mounts as heavy as that at such speed. It's got to be the Militia."

Without delay they set off again spurring the horse to renewed efforts. They clattered down the steep hill into Tregony at breakneck speed, narrowly avoiding an accident on the sharp hairpin turns before the river. Tregony had built up a thriving market in farm machinery with a number of routes converging on the village, with luck their tracks would be lost amongst the numerous ruts that converged on each other, like a spider's web. They pressed on up the hill to the west. Half way up, the gallant pony could pull no more and ground to a halt. John leapt out and grabbed the reins. Painfully slowly the cart began to move again. The distant sound of hooves was getting closer. They reached level ground and the pony was able to take the weight again. John drove the animal to its limits, spurred on by the voices that could clearly be heard as the Militia searched the village.

John handed the reins to Meg.

"Take these. I will see you in Gorran Haven. There should be a boat waiting to take you out to the ship. If I am not there by 12 o'clock, go without me."

"But..."

"No buts, just do as I say."

Meg took the reins and John disappeared into the darkness.

The pony plodded on through the darkness, Meg trusting to hope that they were travelling in the right direction. She heard shouts from behind but pushed on relentlessly, bouncing the cart over the ruts causing Jan to bite deep into his lip with pain.

The shouting continued but did not seem to be getting any nearer. They seemed to be concentrating their search on the banks of the river.

At last Meg caught the outline of the sea shimmering in the moonlight. On and on she went until they reached the top of the hill that led from Gorran village to the harbour below. The descent was tricky. The cart that had proved such a weight for the pony, now posed an even bigger threat as it threatened to career out of control. Half way down Meg managed to stop the cart and jam a stone under the wheel.

"Jan, can you hear me?" She asked urgently.

The wound to Jan's shoulder was bleeding again. He groaned through the pain and opened his eyes.

"We shall have to walk the last bit, can you do it?"

"Of course," he replied. Mustering all his strength he rolled out of the cart grimacing with pain.

Meg rushed to his side and together they half fell and half stumbled down to the harbour. She looked around frantically, of the boatman there was no sign. It was quarter before twelve.

Shouts echoed around the far side of the harbour and the sound of running feet could clearly be heard. Meg dragged Jan into the shadows by the harbour wall.

Out of the shadow a voice whispered.

Do 'ee be John Carter?"

Meg jumped out of her skin. The figure came closer and Meg could pick out the gnarled features of a sea-faring man. She stared at him suspiciously.

"We are friends of John Carter. Are you the man who is to take us to meet The Queen of the Isles?"

"My business is with John Carter."

"John will be here soon."

He came a step closer. Meg could see the brooding, suspicious eyes common with a number of the Celtic breed.

"'Tis a risk I'm running especially with soldiers nearby."

"You will be well paid for your trouble," Meg replied sharply. "Now can you help me get this injured man onto your boat."

Reluctantly he lifted Jan off the ground and together they carried him across the sand to the lee of the quay wall where a small boat had been beached. The man untied the rope and prepared to push the boat into the water.

"No! Wait! John said twelve o'clock- we still have five minutes."

"God dang it, maid! There's soldiers over there, haven't I taken enough risks already?"

Meg summoned up all her womanly charms. "Just another five minutes, please!"

The old man grumbled and cursed but he did not cast off.

They both gazed intently towards the road out of the Haven. Nothing.

"He ain't comin," he said finally and set about untying the mooring rope.

Suddenly, from the other side of the quay there was the sound of running.

"Over here John," Meg called desperately.

The figure headed to where they were. Behind him was a tall figure gaining with every stride.

"Halt, John Carter, or I fire."

There was no escape. The tall man was pointing a musket right at John's head.

John realising the game was up stood panting beside the boat.

"So, John Carter and Jan Pendray."

Jan, who had levered himself up from the deck of the boat, recognised the voice instantly.

"Sergeant Crowlas- we meet again."

The tall Sergeant had dreamt of this moment ever since the humiliation he had received at the hands of Jan Pendray. One shout from him and the whole troop of Militia would descend on the most wanted men in the County of Cornwall. But he couldn't do it.

Gritting his teeth he signalled to the boatman to cast off.

"You have two minutes, go now."

They scrambled into the boat without a second bidding.

"I shall remember this Sergeant Crowlas," gasped John. "You have proved that there is still some humanity left in this County of ours."

"Conscience, Sergeant Crowlas, conscience," said Jan weakly as the boat nosed gently away from the Harbour wall.

They watched the tall figure stand motionless as his quarry slipped into the darkness.

"Why did he let us go?" Meg asked incredulously.

"He's like us in many ways," said Jan. "He wants what's best for the law-abiding people of Cornwall. It was his way of getting back at Peter Pendennis. I don't think the Sergeant will grieve for too long that he let his quarry escape."

The lanterns of the Queen of the Isles shone brightly as the tiny boat brought its cargo safely to the rigging that had been slung over the side. Bidding the old man farewell they clambered up the rigging with Jan holding on for dear life with his one good arm. As the ship slipped its anchor they stood on the deck and watched the familiar coastline disappear over the horizon. Tears ran unashamedly down their faces as they bid farewell to their home and set about thinking of the life they were about to lead in the New Country.

END OF BOOK ONE

Printed in Great Britain
by Amazon

10278163R00093